Mayday Mania!

Clint and Angela were flattened against a wall on the second deck as people ran by. The majority of the passengers did not seem to have grasped the gravity of the situation. They were still running to and fro rather than abandoning ship. People were being knocked off their feet and trampled.

Clint helped an older woman to her feet before she got trampled and said to her, "You have to jump overboard."

She stared at him as if he was crazy, shook loose, and started running.

"You can't help everyone, Clint," Angela said. "We have to save ourselves."

"All right," he said. "Let's get off this thing."

They had to push through a wave of people in order to get to the rail.

"Can you swim?" he asked her.

"I don't know," she said honestly. "I guess we're about to find out."

P9-CAR-079

**DON'T MISS THESE
ALL-ACTION WESTERN SERIES
FROM THE BERKLEY PUBLISHING GROUP**

THE GUNSMITH by J. R. Roberts
Clint Adams was a legend among lawmen, outlaws, and ladies. They called him . . . the Gunsmith.

LONGARM by Tabor Evans
The popular long-running series about Deputy U.S. Marshal Custis Long—his life, his loves, his fight for justice.

SLOCUM by Jake Logan
Today's longest-running action Western. John Slocum rides a deadly trail of hot blood and cold steel.

BUSHWHACKERS by B. J. Lanagan
An action-packed series by the creators of Longarm! The rousing adventures of the most brutal gang of cutthroats ever assembled—Quantrill's Raiders.

DIAMONDBACK by Guy Brewer
Dex Yancey is Diamondback, a Southern gentleman turned con man when his brother cheats him out of the family fortune. Ladies love him. Gamblers hate him. But nobody pulls one over on Dex . . .

WILDGUN by Jack Hanson
The blazing adventures of mountain man Will Barlow—from the creators of Longarm!

TEXAS TRACKER by Tom Calhoun
J.T. Law: the most relentless—and dangerous—manhunter in all Texas. Where sheriffs and posses fail, he's the best man to bring in the most vicious outlaws—for a price.

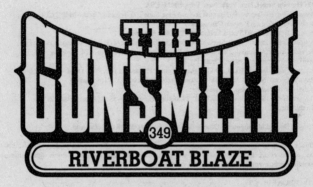

THE GUNSMITH

349

RIVERBOAT BLAZE

J. R. ROBERTS

JOVE BOOKS, NEW YORK

THE BERKLEY PUBLISHING GROUP
Published by the Penguin Group
Penguin Group (USA) Inc.
375 Hudson Street, New York, New York 10014, USA
Penguin Group (Canada), 90 Eglinton Avenue East, Suite 700, Toronto, Ontario M4P 2Y3, Canada
(a division of Pearson Penguin Canada Inc.)
Penguin Books Ltd., 80 Strand, London WC2R 0RL, England
Penguin Group Ireland, 25 St. Stephen's Green, Dublin 2, Ireland (a division of Penguin Books Ltd.)
Penguin Group (Australia), 250 Camberwell Road, Camberwell, Victoria 3124, Australia
(a division of Pearson Australia Group Pty. Ltd.)
Penguin Books India Pvt. Ltd., 11 Community Centre, Panchsheel Park, New Delhi—110 017, India
Penguin Group (NZ), 67 Apollo Drive, Rosedale, North Shore 0632, New Zealand
(a division of Pearson New Zealand Ltd.)
Penguin Books (South Africa) (Pty.) Ltd., 24 Sturdee Avenue, Rosebank, Johannesburg 2196,
South Africa

Penguin Books Ltd., Registered Offices: 80 Strand, London WC2R 0RL, England

This is a work of fiction. Names, characters, places, and incidents either are the product of the author's imagination or are used fictitiously, and any resemblance to actual persons, living or dead, business establishments, events, or locales is entirely coincidental.

RIVERBOAT BLAZE

A Jove Book / published by arrangement with the author

PRINTING HISTORY
Jove edition / January 2011

Copyright © 2011 by Robert J. Randisi.
Cover illustration by Sergio Giovine.

All rights reserved.
No part of this book may be reproduced, scanned, or distributed in any printed or electronic form without permission. Please do not participate in or encourage piracy of copyrighted materials in violation of the author's rights. Purchase only authorized editions.
For information, address: The Berkley Publishing Group,
a division of Penguin Group (USA) Inc.,375 Hudson Street, New York, New York 10014.

ISBN: 978-0-515-14883-1

JOVE®
Jove Books are published by The Berkley Publishing Group,
a division of Penguin Group (USA) Inc.,
375 Hudson Street, New York, New York 10014.
JOVE® is a registered trademark of Penguin Group (USA) Inc.
The "J" design is a trademark of Penguin Group (USA) Inc.

PRINTED IN THE UNITED STATES OF AMERICA

10 9 8 7 6 5 4 3 2 1

If you purchased this book without a cover, you should be aware that this book is stolen property. It was reported as "unsold and destroyed" to the publisher, and neither the author nor the publisher has received any payment for this "stripped book."

ONE

The *Dolly Madison* was the biggest, most well-built riverboat Clint Adams had ever been on. That's why it was such a shock when it started sinking.

But that came later . . .

"It's called the *Dolly Madison*," Dean Dillon said. "It's the biggest stern wheeler ever made, over seven hundred feet long."

"I thought the *Great Eastern* was the biggest," Clint said.

"It was," Dillon said, "or rather, it is, until we take our maiden voyage. Our paddle wheel is sixty feet in diameter. The *Great Eastern* is only fifty-seven. We weigh thirty-three thousand tons!"

"When is the big day?"

"A week," Dillon said.

"From where?"

"New Orleans," Dillon said. "And I want you to be on it."

"Oh, uh, Dean—"

"On the house!" Dillon hurriedly added. "You're my friend, Clint, I want you to share this with me."

Clint thought it was more likely Dean was trying to get some big names lined up for his boat's maiden voyage. Not that he could blame him. If Dean had the largest paddle wheeler on the Mississippi, it was going to be a major accomplishment.

"You got anything better to do?" Dillon asked.

Clint studied his friend's face. Dillon had come all the way to Labyrinth, Texas, to invite Clint in person. Maybe the friend in him did want to share the experience with Clint, but the businessman wanted the Gunsmith on that boat.

"Whataya say, Clint?" Dillon asked.

"When are you leaving?" Clint asked.

"Tomorrow morning." Dillon had only arrived that morning. "I'm heading right back."

"Okay," Clint said. "Before you leave, I'll let you know if I can make it."

"Okay," Dillon said. "I'll accept that."

He finished his beer and put the empty mug down on the table.

"See you in the morning," he said. "Stage leaves at nine."

He turned and left Rick's Place, the batwings swinging in his wake.

Rick Hartman came over and sat in the chair Dillon had just vacated.

"So, what did he want?" he asked Clint. "He came running in here like his ass was on fire."

"I'm invited to be on the maiden voyage of the *Dolly Madison*, the largest paddle wheeler ever to hit the Mississippi."

"He owns it?"

"Apparently."

"Then it'll probably sink."

"Well," Clint said, frowning, "did you know that a paddle wheeler can weigh as much as thirty-three thousand tons? How the hell does something that big manage to stay afloat?"

"You got me," Rick said. "I've never liked boats, myself. Trains, yeah, but boats?"

"I do like them," Clint said. "At least, I did until I learned how much they weigh."

"So, are you gonna go?" Hartman asked, sitting back in his chair.

"I don't know," Clint said. "I like New Orleans, I like the Mississippi, I *liked* riverboats—maybe I still do, despite their weight."

"When is this historical voyage supposed to take place?"

"In a week."

"And do you have any other plans?"

"No."

"Then why wouldn't you go?"

"Well," Clint said, "it is Dean Dillon."

"There you go!" Hartman said, with a smile. "It's a scam. It's got to be."

Dean Dillon had been—in no particular order—a gambler, a con man, a thief, a liar, and a businessman. Whichever one he put his mind to at any given moment, he was a damned good one.

The question was—which one was he being now?

TWO

The deck pitched and Angela DuBois, standing next to him, almost fell, and would have if he hadn't caught her.

"Jesus," she said, eyes wide with fright, "we're really going down?"

"Looks like it," Clint said.

People were running back and forth on the deck. Crew members were trying to shout instructions to the passengers, but they were panicked and weren't having any of it. And then, suddenly, there was fire.

"W-what do we do?" she asked.

Clint took her by the shoulders and looked into her eyes.

"Can you swim?"

* * *

FIVE DAYS EARLIER . . .

When Clint arrived in New Orleans, he breathed in its
scent. New Orleans was a special place, unlike any
other city in the United States. The architecture was
French, the population was cross-cultural and multi-
lingual. He loved the people and the food.

He stopped at the Jean Lafitte Hotel, put Eclipse
up at the hotel's livery, and got himself a room.

"Ah, Mr. Adams," the clerk said, "we've been expectin' you, suh."

"You have?"

"Your room is taken care of," the clerk said. He
was very Southern, in his thirties, well-groomed, and
probably better educated than most desk clerks in the
West.

"By who?"

"Mr. Dillon, suh," the clerk said. "He left strict instructions that your money is no good here. Everything will be paid for by him."

"That's very nice of him," Clint said.

"Yes, suh."

A bellboy came over and grabbed Clint's carpetbag. He had decided a trip to New Orleans was worth
more than just his saddlebags packed with a couple of
extra shirts.

Clint followed the boy to his room, which turned
out to be a two-room suite. Dillon must have been
doing real well. Or he was showing off.

"Thank you," Clint said, tipping the boy and usher-
ing him out of the room.

He went to his window, which overlooked Bourbon Street. He was trying to decide what restaurant to eat in when there was a knock on the door. He walked to it and opened it with his gun in his hand.

"'Bout time you got here," Dillon said, barging in. "I got people for you to meet."

"Nice to see you, too, Dean," Clint said. "Thanks for the room."

"Nice, huh?" Dillon asked. "Top of the line for you, Clint."

"Dean, I've already agreed to be on your boat," Clint reminded him.

"And that's why you're gettin' treated so well," Dillon said. "Come on, you must be hungry."

"I am."

"I got some people waitin' at a restaurant down the street, it's called Remoulades."

"What is that, somebody's name?"

"No, I think it's some kind of sauce," Dillon said. "Come on, time's wastin'."

Dillon was wearing a white suit and white fedora. Clint was in trail clothes.

"Don't you think I ought to change into something clean?" Clint asked.

"Well, make it quick," Dillon said. "I got people waitin'.'

Clint went into the other room to wash up and change.

He had nothing like Dillon's white suit, but he did have clean trousers and shirt. He also kept his gun on.

"You really need that?" Dillon asked, as they walked along the paved sidewalk.

"Have you met me?" Clint asked.

"Yeah, okay," Dillon said, "but try not to shoot any-body."

"I'll give it my best shot."

Dillon took Clint down to the street, where they walked two blocks to the restaurant.

"Who are the people we're meeting?" he asked, as they walked.

"Investors," Dillon said, "other passengers. Friends. Don't worry, I'll introduce you to everyone."

Clint grabbed Dillon's arm, halting their progress down the busy street.

"Dean, don't introduce me as the Gunsmith," he said. "Introduce me by name."

"Somebody's gonna know you're the Gunsmith, Clint," Dillon said.

"That's okay," he said. "Let them ask. I'll answer them."

"Okay," Dillon said, "whatever you say."

THREE

They continued on and Clint followed Dillon into Remoulades. It was busy, all the tables occupied. Dillon led him to the back of the room, where there was a table for twelve holding ten people at the moment.

"Hey, there's our host!" somebody yelled.

"I thought you were gonna stick us with the bill, Dean," another man called out.

"Not a chance," Dillon said, sliding in to sit next to a blond woman. That left one seat for Clint, across from the woman.

"Hey, baby," Dillon said. He leaned over and kissed the woman's cheek, but she was looking at Clint.

"Clint, this is Angela," Dillon said. "Best damn blackjack dealer on the Mississippi. Baby, meet my good friend Clint Adams."

"Happy to meet you, Mr. Adams," she said. Clint guessed she was in her late twenties, a girl just coming into womanhood.

"Down the table you got Hal Miller, Danny Rawlins, and Bill Kennedy. They're my investors."

"And our money is safe with you, right, Dean?" Miller asked.

"Safe as can be, Hal," Dillon said.

Miller and Rawlins were in their forties, Kennedy about ten years older than that. They were all well-dressed, looked like businessmen.

"Across from them are some of our passengers," Dillon said. "Troy Galvin, poker player."

Galvin, a handsome man in his thirties, inclined his head a few inches.

"That's his lady next to him, uh . . ."

"Kathy," she said.

"Yeah, sorry," Dillon said, "Kathy."

Kathy had a pretty if sullen face, looked about twenty-five, and didn't seem very happy to be there.

"Then we've got Johnny Kingdom—"

"I've heard of Johnny Kingdom," Clint said.

"I'm flattered," Kingdom said. He was in his late thirties and had had a reputation in poker circles for about ten years. "I've heard of you, too, Mr. Adams. The Gunsmith, right?"

Dillon gave him an "I told you so" look.

"That's right," Clint said.

"Oh really?" Angela said, looking at him with even more interest.

"Is Mr. Adams going to be a passenger?" another man asked. He was so slender his clothes looked too big for him. And his hands shook. Clint didn't know if he was nervous, or if they shook for another reason.

He was also sweaty, and held a white handkerchief in his hand, which he used to wipe his brow.

"Yes, Mr. Corso, Clint is gonna be a passenger," Dillon said.

"T-that's good to hear," Corso said. "I mean, that you hired a man like the Gunsmith for security."

"I'm not for hire, Mr. Corso," Clint said.

"That's right," Dillon said. "Clint is coming at my invitation. We've been friends for a long time."

"I see," Corso said. "Still . . ." He didn't finish his sentence.

There were three more people to be introduced, two men and a woman. They were passengers. The men were brothers, Sam and Lou Warrant. The woman, although she was sitting between them, did not seem to be with them. She was introduced as Ava Cantrell.

She leaned across Lou Warrant to shake Clint's hand.

"Pleased to meet you, Mr. Adams."

"My pleasure, Miss Cantrell."

She had black hair and thick, luxurious lips.

"Ava is our singer," Dillon said. "Sam and Lou . . . well, they're friends of mine."

The Warrant brothers looked to be in their twenties, and if Clint was any judge, they *were* for hire. Even though Dillon was introducing them as friends.

They both nodded at Clint. He leaned back and was able to ascertain that they were wearing holsters on their hips. A couple of the other men—Kingdom and Galvin—obviously had guns beneath their jackets. The three businessmen—Dillon's investors—did not seem to be armed.

If any of the three women had guns, they were not readily evident.

"Now that we all know each other, let's have some drinks," Dillon said.

"We're here to find out the details of our boat's first cruise, Dean," Miller said.

"Sure, sure, we'll go over that," Dillon said. "I'll tell everybody when to be there. But first let's get some drinks for the table. Waiter!"

A waiter came over and took drink orders. Clint noticed that Dillon ordered for both Angela and Ava. He also noticed that both women were looking at him, while the men at the table were looking at them. Kathy seemed to grow more and more sullen.

Clint ordered a beer.

FOUR

While they had their drinks, they got acquainted, although it was hard for Clint to talk to anyone but Dillon, who was on his left, and Lou Warrant, on his right. When Ava wanted to speak to him, she'd lean across Lou, who didn't seem to mind at all.

Angela sat across from Clint, eyeing him in a way that made him nervous. If she was Dillon's woman, then they were headed for trouble.

Or maybe Ava was his woman. Either way there'd be trouble. He'd have to talk to Dillon about it before he got on the boat.

Over a second round of drinks Dillon told everyone when to be at the docks to either see the boat off or get on board. Apparently, none of the three investors was going to be on board. Clint wondered if that was because they weren't all that confident about how safe the big boat was. Maybe, like Clint, they had found out how much the boat really weighed.

After about an hour the three businessmen left. After that Troy Galvin and his sullen girlfriend Kathy left, saying they'd see Dillon on the boat.

That left Dillon, Clint, Angela, Ava, Johnny Kingdom, and the Warrant brothers.

"We're all gonna be on that boat," Dillon said. "And we're gonna be family."

"Family?" Clint asked.

"Sam and Lou work for me. So do Angela and Ava."

"And Johnny?" Clint asked. He looked at Kingdom.

"I don't work for Dean," Kingdom said, "but we do have an arrangement."

"Well, I don't work for you," Clint said to Dean.

"No, you don't," Dillon said, "but you're my guest."

"What about Galvin? And his girl?"

"You call that a girl?" Angela asked. "More like a mouse."

"She's nice," Ava said, "just a little shy."

"You friends with her?" Angela asked.

"Not friends," Ava said. "We just talked."

"Let's have another drink," Dillon said.

"Not me," Clint said. "I'm going to walk around a bit. It's been a while since I've been in New Orleans."

"Will you walk me?" Ava asked.

"Where do you want to go, Ava?" Kingdom asked. "I'll walk you."

"No," Ava said, standing up, "I'll go with Clint. You stay here with Dean and the boys." Clint noticed that Ava had not referred to Angela. He had a feeling the two women would never be friends.

"Will you walk me?" she asked Clint.

"Sure." He looked at Dillon. "Dean, see you at the boat."

"That's two days, Clint," Dillon said. "Let's have dinner tonight."

"Tomorrow night," Clint said. "I want to spend a day in the city."

"Okay, then," Dillon said. "Tomorrow night. Meet me at Jacques' at seven."

"I'll be there."

"So will I," Angela said.

"Yeah, baby, you'll be there," Dillon said to her.

"See you then," Clint said to both of them.

Clint walked out with Ava hanging onto his arm.

"Where do you want to go, Ava?" he asked when they were on the street.

"Wherever you want to go," she said, squeezing his arm.

"I thought you had to go somewhere," he said.

"Well, I wanted to get out of there," she said. "Johnny Kingdom had his hands on me under the table. And I don't like Angela."

"You were sitting between the Warrant brothers," he said.

"Well, then maybe it was Sam's hands," she said. She slid her arm from his. "I just wanted to get out of there, with you."

"Why me?"

She shrugged. "Why not?"

Now it was Clint's turn to shrug.

"Okay, then," he said. "Let's go."

"Where?"

"I want to go over to Jackson Square," he told her,

"take a look at St. Louis Cathedral, maybe have some
jambalaya."

"I know a great place for jambalaya," she said.

"Well, all right, then," he said. He took her hand,
looped it back inside his arm. "Let's go."

FIVE

She did, indeed, know a place for some great jamba-laya. They stopped there after going to Jackson Square, stopping in St. Louis Cathedral, walking down by the river. They talked the whole time. Clint found out that she was twenty-four, from New Orleans, had been singing in bars there for years. Her father was white, but her mother was Creole, so she was a half-breed. He figured that was where she came by her coffee-colored skin, and her luscious thick lips, and those big brown eyes. She could pass as white if she wanted to, but she never lied about her background.

"I ain't ashamed of it," she said.

"You shouldn't be," he said. "Do you sing as good as you look?"

She laughed and asked, "How good do I look?"

"Damn good," he said. "You're a beautiful girl, Ava. You know that."

They were walking down Bourbon Street as the

light began to fade, and she said, "If you take me to your room, I'll let you see how good I really look."

That was an offer he couldn't pass up.

Dean Dillon's hotel was smaller than Clint's, but more expensive. It was also closer to the docks.

Down in the bar he sat with the Warrant brothers and Angela.

"What about Adams?" Sam asked.

"What about him?"

"Is he gonna help or not?" Lou asked.

"He's my friend," Dillon said. "If there's any trouble, he'll be there. But don't forget who I'm payin' to provide security."

"Us," Sam said.

"That's right."

The Warrants reached out for their drinks.

"You boys can go now. Angela and I want to be alone."

They stopped short of their glasses, exchanged a glance, then grabbed their drinks, stood up, and walked away.

"We want to be alone?" she asked.

"Don't we?" he asked.

"I'm a dealer," she said, "not a whore."

He smiled, put his hand on her leg, and replied, "Who said I was gonna pay you?"

As Clint closed the door, Ava moved to the center of the room. There was only a little light left outside, but it was enough to see her. He started to reach for the gas lamp on the wall.

"No," she said, turning, "leave it."

"I want to see you," he said.

She smiled.

"You will see me," she said.

The dress she wore had a scooped neck, but only showed a bit of her cleavage. However, it clung to her closely enough to outline large melon-shaped breasts. She seemed to need only to shrug her shoulders for the garment to fall to the floor. Next, a wisp of fabric from around her waist, and she was naked.

Gloriously so.

Clint had read some books about the Greek gods and goddesses. He thought that what he was seeing now could not be any les beautiful than a Greek goddess. He literally felt breathless while looking at her.

She raised her arms and twirled around for him. Her dark skin was flawless, her breasts perfect. She had dark brown nipples and a wild pubic thatch, as pitch-black as the hair on her head. There was also some dark hair in her armpits, which only served to make her even more appealing to him.

"Can you see me?" she asked.

"Oh," he said, "I can see you."

She stopped twirling and faced him, lowering her arms.

"And now it's my turn," she said.

He unbuckled his gun and set it down nearby. He wanted to tear his clothes off, but he didn't want to seem too anxious, so he undressed slowly. By the time he removed his underwear, though, he was fully aroused, and she caught her breath as his penis rose up and pointed at her.

She walked across the room, confronted him, took his penis into both hands.

"I spend a lot of time naked," she said.

"Not in public, I hope."

She laughed. "No, but whenever I am in private, I like it," she said. "And it suits you."

She backed toward the bed, maintaining her hold on him. He had no choice but to follow.

But he would have, anyway.

SIX

Ava was almost as tall as Clint. She was a lot of woman, and Clint felt like the luckiest man alive when he took her into his arms and kissed her. She had a natural, musky odor about her that permeated his nostrils. He kissed her mouth, then her neck and shoulders, finally moving down to her breasts. He took them in his hands, caressed them while he kissed and licked the turgid nipples. Her skin was hot and smooth. As he bit her, she moaned, slid her hands into his hair, holding him tightly to her bosom.

He let his hands roam over her body, and she suddenly, impatiently grabbed him and took him down to the bed with amazing strength. Once on the mattress, she wrangled him onto his back and straddled him, trapping his penis between them. She rubbed her furry patch up and down the length of him, bracing herself with her hands flat against his chest. He began to move his hips with her, and soon they were both slick with her juices. Finally, she lifted her hips and allowed him to slide right into her, then she sat down hard on him, taking him all the way in.

The light waned, and she became just a silhouette rising and falling on him, slickly, wetly, hotly. She started to moan, and her moans turned to grunts each time she came down on him.

He found her rhythm and started moving with her, sliding his hands up over his breasts, around behind her to her beautiful back. She leaned forward then so he could reach her breasts and nipples with his mouth. In that position he was able to slide his hand beneath her buttocks. She soaked them both with her juices, which smelled both sweet and sharp. In fact, the smell became so intoxicating that Clint also wanted a taste.

He tried to turn her, and for a moment they wrestled, both grunting with the effort, but finally he got her onto her back and slid down between her legs. He parted the curtain of hair with his fingers, then probed with his tongue. He began to lap at her, tasting her sweetness, causing her hips to jerk and a gasp to come from her mouth each time he touched her. Once again she reached for him, wrapped his hair in her fingers, and held him there. At one point she was even rubbing his face into her crotch, and he thought she was almost strong enough to hold him there and drown him in her wetness.

He slid his hands beneath her buttocks again, cupped them, and lifted her so that he was in control of her. As he continued to lick and suck her, she released his head so she could beat her fists on the mattress and then take handfuls of the sheets.

Finally, she trembled and then cried out as she once again gushed and—in a sharp reversal—started to push him away while her orgasm overtook her . . .

Dillon walked Angela to her room.

"How about a nightcap?" he asked.

"We just had a nightcap," she said. "In fact, several."

"Then how about just asking me in?"

"No," she said. "What about your Creole singer?"

"Ava? She just works for me."

"So do I."

What's goin' on, Angela?" he asked. "I thought this was where we were headin'."

"Maybe," she said, unlocking her door, "it's just taken too long to get here. Good night, Dean."

She went into her room and closed the door in his face.

Shaking his head, he turned and walked down the hall.

Inside the room, Angela leaned against the door and listened to Dean Dillon's retreating footsteps. Maybe she and Dean were heading here, but that all changed when Clint Adams sat across from her. Now he was probably with that Creole bitch, who had thrown herself at him like the bitch in heat that she was, but that would change. Once they were on the boat, that would change.

Clint didn't allow Ava any time to regain her breath. He turned her over, receiving little or no resistance this time. He lifted her up onto all fours, then slid his hard dick up between her thighs and into her. She gasped and shuddered, and then he began taking her, first in long, easy strokes, but little by little increasing the tempo, until he was slamming himself into her and she was crying out.

Once she found his rhythm, she began to slam back against him as he drove into her, and pretty soon the familiar sound of flesh slapping flesh filled the room.

SEVEN

THE PRESENT

The fire began to spread . . .

"Clint," Angela said, holding his arm tightly. "What's happening?"

"I don't know," he said. "Have you seen Dean or Ava?"

"No."

"The Warrant brothers?"

"I thought I saw Sam go overboard."

"Fall overboard?"

She shook her head. "It looked to me like he jumped."

"Then Lou probably went over first," Clint said. "Those two do everything together."

"What do we do?" she asked.

The boat listed heavily to one side again, and he

said, "I think we're going to have to do the same thing, Angela. This boat is going down."

"But . . . that's supposed to be impossible."

"Yeah," he said. "I know."

THREE DAYS EARLIER . . .

Clint looked up at the *Dolly Madison* from the dock. It was an impressive boat, no question about it.

"What do you think?"

He turned. It was Miller, one of the backers.

"Impressive," Clint said.

"Big," Miller said.

"Why aren't you going?" Clint asked. "You and your partners?"

"Like I said," Miller answered, "big. I don't see how something like this can even float."

"I know what you mean," Clint said. "When Dean told me how much it weighed—"

"Don't tell me," Miller said. "I don't want to know."

"Guess I can't blame you."

"Hello, Clint."

He turned and saw Ava, looking lovely in a blue dress and shawl. Her short black hair was kind of spiky, as if all she had done that morning was run her fingers through it.

They had spent a day together, but not last night. They both had to get their belongings ready to move to the boat. Dillon had their bags picked up for them in the morning.

"Good morning, Ava," Clint said.

"Mr. Miller," Ava said.

"Hello, Ava," Miller said, looking uncomfortable. "I'll, uh, I have some things to do. Nice to see you, Adams."

They both watched the man walk away.

"He doesn't like Creole people," she said.

"You're only half-Creole," Clint said.

"He can't tell the difference," she said. "Have you seen Dean this morning?"

"No, not yet. Maybe he's on board."

"Will you escort me aboard?" she asked.

He put his arm out and said, "It will be my pleasure."

They walked up the gangway together.

From the deck Sam and Lou Warrant watched Clint and Ava walk onto the boat together.

"Think he's gonna be a problem?" Sam asked.

"Naw," Lou said. "He don't know what's goin' on, and he's gonna be busy sniffin' around Ava."

"I aim to do some of that sniffin' myself," Sam said.

"Not me," Lou said. "I'm gonna be sniffin' around Angela."

"Don't like blond hair," Sam said.

"Don't matter," Lou said, "'cause I'm gonna have her facin' the other way."

"Hey," Sam said, "maybe we can do that together."

"You said you don't like blondes."

"Well," Sam said, "if she's facin' the other way . . ."

The Warrant brothers were on the second deck, watching Clint and Ava enter on the first deck.

Up on the third deck Dean Dillon was looking

down on everything. This had to turn out right, he thought. Not only did he have investors to answer to, but he had all his own money tied up in the *Dolly Madison*. That was why he wanted Clint on board. He knew if there was any trouble, the Gunsmith would be able to handle it.

"How's it look, Boss?"

Dillon turned and looked at his second in command, Mike Chambers.

"Everything's goin' smoothly, so far," he said. "I have to talk to the captain. Why don't you stay here and watch things."

"Sure, Boss."

Dillon took one last look around, then turned and walked to the wheelhouse.

EIGHT

Clint was standing on the deck with Ava when Dean Dillon finally appeared.

"'Mornin', you two. Glad you made it."

"Dean," Clint said. "We were wondering how we were going to find our way to our cabins."

"That'll be me," Dillon said. "I'll show you both, but let's wait a minute. I see Angela coming up the gangway."

Clint looked and saw the pretty blonde making her way on board.

"I know where my cabin is," Ava said. "I'll see you boys later."

After she left, Clint asked, "What was that about?"

"I'm afraid the ladies don't get along," Dean said.

"Why is that?"

"Who knows, with women?" Dillon asked. "You'll have to ask them. "Mornin', Angela."

"Good morning, gents," she said. "Beautiful day for it, Dean."

"Yes, it is," Dillon said. "You look lovely this mornin'."

"Thank you. Where's Ava?"

"She's on her way to her cabin," Dillon said. "Why don't I show the two of you to yours?"

"I'm ready," Angela said.

"So am I," Clint said.

"This way."

They went inside and Dillon led them to a stairway.

"You're both on the third deck, Angela because she's working for me, and you, Clint, because you're a guest." Dillon pointedly looked at Clint and said, "Ava's also on this level."

"What about the Warrant brothers?" Clint said.

"I've got them on two," Dillon said. "Employees who hate sharing cabins are on two."

He led them to a door with a "1" on it and said, "This is Angela. Clint, you're down the way in number five. It should be unlocked."

"Thanks, Dean. Angela. See you both later."

"Once we get under way, we'll have some food and champagne served to celebrate," Dillon said. "That'll be just outside here. So I'll see you both then."

"Fine," Clint said.

Dillon stood still in front of Angela's door, so Clint excused himself, walked down to his cabin, and let himself in. It wasn't large, but it was pretty nice, easily the best cabin he'd ever had on a riverboat. He dropped his carpetbag in a corner, leaned his rifle against the wall, then went to look out the single window. He could see all the activity on the dock as people boarded, materials were loaded, as well as stock. Clint had chosen to leave Eclipse in the Jean Lafitte's stable, rather than take the horse on board. For one thing Eclipse had never been on a riverboat before, so Clint didn't know how the Darley Arabian gelding would take it. And second, all somebody had to do was tell Clint a boat was unsinkable to make him start to worry. He felt better leaving Eclipse on dry land.

It would take a while for everything to get loaded and for them to get under way, so he sat down on the bed and opened his carpetbag. There was a chest of drawers against one wall, and he started to put his belongings in there.

Suddenly, there was a knock on his door. He walked to it and opened it with his hand on his gun.

When he opened the door, Angela came rushing in.

"Quick, before somebody sees me!" she said.

He closed the door.

"Angela, what's wrong?"

"Nothing," she said. "The way I figure it, you spent at least one night with Ava this week, maybe two."

"Um, well—"

"So I wanted to state my case as early as I could when we got on board."

Abruptly, she began to unbutton her dress.

"Whoa, Angela," he said. "What's going on?"

"It's going to be a while before we can get under way," she said, pulling the dress down. "Nobody will bother us for a while."

She must have planned this well ahead of time,

because she hadn't worn any underwear. Her pale skin came into view, smooth and flawless. Her breasts were small but seemed solid, like ripe peaches, with pink nipples. She hopped on one foot to get the dress off, and then the other, which made her taut breasts jiggle nicely.

Finally, she was naked, and she stood that way in front of him. Between her legs there seemed to be a pelt of gold.

"Well?" she asked. "Are you going to reject me? Put me out into the hall naked?"

"I'm not going to do either of those things," Clint said. "I'm going to lock the door."

NINE

Mike Chambers watched as a huge crate was loaded onto the riverboat. He noticed it because it seemed to be the heaviest crate they were carrying that day.

"What's up?" Dillon asked, coming up alongside Chambers. "You look worried."

"You sure we can carry everything we've contracted to carry, Dean?" Chambers asked. "I mean, look at that crate." He pointed.

Dillon looked down at the crate, which was being swung on board.

"I looked that crate over myself," he said. "The shipper is traveling with us. We're takin' it to St. Louis."

"We're goin' that far?" Chambers asked.

"And farther," Dillon said, with a nod. "We're going all the way."

"Minnesota?"

Dillon nodded.

Chambers banged his hand on the wooden railing, found no give in it.

"Is the rest of the boat really built this good?" he asked.

"Mike, are you doubting me? You've seen the plans for this boat."

"Yeah, I know," Chambers said. "Biggest boat on the Mississippi."

"Biggest and best," Dillon said. He slapped Chambers on his broad shoulders. "Don't worry so much."

"That's my job," Chambers said. "To worry."

"I'm not worried, Mike," Dillon said.

"I know," Chambers said, "and the less you worry, the more I do. Like I said, that's my job."

"Okay, Mike," Dillon said. "You keep doin' your job. I'm gonna go down to the dock and greet the rest of my guests."

Chambers looked at the dock and saw Troy Galvin with his girlfriend, Kathy.

"I don't like that guy," he said.

"We needed some gamblers, Mike," Dillon said. "Kingdom was the only big name I could get, so I had to settle for Galvin."

"Not crazy about Kingdom, either," Chambers admitted.

This time Dillon slapped Chambers on the back.

"Take it easy, Mike. The gamblers ain't what you should be worrying about."

Dillon went down to the docks while Chambers remained where he was, watching the action.

* * *

Clint's time with Angela was different from his time with Ava. Ava was a sexual predator, and he had been her prey. Though he had managed to turn the tables during their time together, the sex had been almost as much of a struggle as it had been a pleasure.

Angela was different. She was gentler, even though she was hurrying them along.

"No time for niceties," she told him, pushing him down on the bed. She straddled him. "I want you to know I'm ready for anything."

"Apparently," he said.

She reached between them for his penis, held it in place, and settled down onto it with a sigh.

"Oh, God," she said. "Mmmmm . . . we have to hurry this time, but next time—"

"There's going to be a next time?"

She closed her eyes and gave herself up to the feeling of him inside of her.

"Oh yes," she almost whispered, "definitely a next time." Then she opened her eyes and looked down at him. "Unless you don't want to?"

He reached up and gently cupped her breasts, thumbing the pink nipples. She moaned.

"Oh, I want to . . ." he said.

Kingdom arrived on the dock before Dillon came down to greet Galvin.

"Kingdom," Galvin said.

"Troy," Kingdom said. "Miss."

"You can call her by her name," Galvin said.

"Kathy," Kingdom said, wondering if that was a test.

"Is this being set up as you against me?" Galvin asked.

"That's not my understanding," Kingdom said.

"Might end up that way."

"It's not a tournament, Galvin," Kingdom said. "My understanding is that we play against the passengers."

"Still," Galvin said, "you never know."

Kingdom looked at Kathy. She smiled a sad smile and looked away. He thought she was probably very pretty when she wasn't sad.

TEN

The positions didn't change much in sex. Not when you had as much experience as Clint had. The only thing that changed was the women, and their attitudes, their approaches, and their experience.

Ava and Angela apparently had age and experience in common. And, in fact, they had both been aggressive in their approaches. The difference came in their execution.

Although Angela stated they had to hurry, her movements were slow and languid. The rush, he assumed, was in the fact that there wouldn't be many more positions than just this one.

But she began to float away the longer they made love. Her eyes closed, her head thrown back, she arched her back, scratched his chest gently, and moaned when he touched her breasts and nipples with his hands or mouth.

The thing that jerked her back to reality was a loud

noise from outside, probably a crate or something that was being loaded.

Her eyes flew open and she looked down at him.

"Welcome back," he said.

"Shit," she said, and increased the tempo of her hips.

Kingdom and Galvin were shown to their cabins on the second level. Kingdom was unpacking when there was a knock on his door. When he opened it and saw Kathy, he wasn't that surprised.

"You're not surprised," she said.

"Do you want to come in?"

"Another time," she said.

"What can I do for you, then?"

"You can beat him."

"Who?"

"Troy," she said. "You can beat him."

"Well, I know that," he said. "If we end up at the same table, the odds are good I'll beat him."

"No, I mean you *can*," she said. "I can help you."

"How?"

"He always likes me with him when he plays," she said. "I can signal you, let you know when he has a weak hand or a strong hand, let you know when he's bluffing or when he's betting from strength. I know the game very well."

"And why would you do that?"

"Because I want to see him beaten," she said. "I want to see him humbled."

"Again I'll ask, why?"

She looked both ways. There were other people

being shown to their cabins, but she didn't seem concerned about them. She was only worried about being seen by Galvin.

Unless, of course, Galvin had sent her.

"You don't trust me," she said. "You think he sent me?"

"I think it's possible."

She fidgeted.

"Look," she said, "I can't stand here forever."

"Come inside."

"I can't," she said. "Think about it. I'll talk to you again when I can."

"Okay," he said, "I'll think about it."

She nodded, turned, and left in a hurry. He didn't have time to ask her where Troy Galvin thought she was.

Angela grunted and moaned her way to her orgasm, then ground her hips down on Clint until he exploded inside of her. Then she hopped off and hurriedly began to dress.

"Okay," she said, "so that can't have been as good as a whole night with Ava, but I just wanted to declare myself."

"You did a good job of it," he said, watching with pleasure as she dressed. It was one of his great pleasures in life.

She sat on the bed and pulled on her boots, then looked over at him. He was lying on his back with his hands behind his neck. His penis had not lost all of its hardness. She reached out and stroked it with her right hand. It twitched, as if it had a mind of its own.

Sometimes it did, and he tried not to let that get him into trouble.

"I have to go," she said.

"Come back anytime."

"I will," she said. "I just hope I don't find Ava here." He shrugged.

"Do you play blackjack?" she asked.

"Not when I can play poker," he said.

"I don't understand poker."

"Really? I'll show you how to play someday."

"Oh, no," she said, "I know how to play the game, I just don't understand the fascination with it."

She stroked him one last time, then walked to the door and left. Clint decided he should get dressed before the boat got under way.

ELEVEN

Clint was out on deck on the third level, watching the last of the passengers board and the gangway being pulled in.

"We're almost ready to get under way," Dillon said, coming up next to him. "Where've you been?"

"In my cabin."

"All this time?"

"I had to unpack."

"All this time?"

Clint looked at Dillon.

"I like my cabin."

"That's good to hear," Dillon said.

"When is this celebration supposed to take place?" Clint asked.

"About a half hour after we disembark," Dillon said. "In the main salon and outside on this deck."

Disembark. Clint wasn't sure Dillon had used that word correctly.

"Okay," Clint said. "I'll be there."

"Unless you get . . . distracted again," Dillon said, with a grin.

"You got something you want to ask me?" Clint said.

"I already asked, and you told me you were un-packing," Dillon said. "I guess Ava was unpacking all that time, too."

As Dillon walked away, Clint was satisfied that the man thought he'd been with Ava. He still wasn't sure what Dillon's relationship with Angela was. He was going to have to ask her.

As Kathy entered the cabin, Galvin said, "There you are." He was standing in the center of the cabin, hold-ing a drink.

"I just needed to get some air."

"You have to unpack for us."

"Okay."

"I need my black suit," he said.

"Which one?"

"Which one do you think?" he demanded. "The one I always wear on the first night."

"Of course."

"I can't find it myself, Kathy," he complained.

She knew that. He was helpless without her, not that he'd ever admit it. But she was growing tired of his dependence. The only way she knew to get out from under him was to make sure he was beaten, and humiliated. She felt Kingdom was the man for that job.

She hoped he was.

* * *

Kingdom had his own agenda.

Play poker.

Win money.

He didn't want to get caught up in Kathy's agenda. And even if he was to beat Galvin at the poker table, he wouldn't want any help to do it.

Actually, Galvin wasn't the one he was thinking about playing. That was Clint Adams. He hoped to get the Gunsmith to the poker table. Not for who he was, but for who he had played poker against. He knew Adams had sat across the table from the likes of Bat Masterson, Luke Short, and Ben Thompson, and held his own. Kingdom wanted to test himself against a man like that.

He knew champagne and food were being served on the third deck as a celebration. He put on a gray suit. He only wore black when he was playing.

He slid his .32 into his shoulder holster and left his cabin.

Clint strapped on his gun and put on his hat. Time for celebrating, but as he opened the door and stepped out he wondered if he had done the right thing even coming here.

He was sure Dillon just wanted his name, but Dillon had also been right. He had nothing better to do, and he hadn't been in New Orleans in a while. He loved this city. The women, the food, the buildings. And then there was Ava . . .

It had been worth coming for the couple of days he'd spent in New Orleans. Now, as long as the weight of this crazy boat didn't take it down, a trip up the Mississippi might be interesting.

He stepped out onto the deck and saw people standing around drinking champagne and eating sandwiches. When he entered the main salon, he saw a lot more than sandwiches laid out. There was quite a bit of New Orleans cuisine on the tables, with waiters walking around carrying trays of champagne in crystal glasses.

He approached the table, saw trays of jambalaya, shrimp, pots of gumbo.

"Impressive, huh?" Dillon asked. "All from our onboard kitchen."

"Is it any good?"

"My cook is the best. I stole him from a restaurant on Bourbon Street."

"Well, I'll let you know what I think."

Dillon grabbed a glass of champagne from a passing waiter and handed it to Clint. "You do that."

He walked away to mingle with his other guests.

"Hey, you," someone said.

He turned and saw Ava holding a glass of champagne.

"Hungry?" she asked.

"For food?"

"What else would I mean?"

He smiled at her, and noticed her eyes shift past him.

"Here comes that bitch Angela."

"What makes her a bitch?" he asked.

She looked at him again and smiled.

"Talk to her," she said. "If you figure out the answer, let me know."

TWELVE

Clint mingled with the other passengers; some recognized his name, some didn't. The ones who did either found it fascinating or shrank away, unsure.

"You're scaring some of my passengers," Dillon said later.

"I'm sure that was part of your plan," Clint said. "To give them something special for the trip?"

"They'll learn that you're harmless," Dillon said. "After all, no one could have earned a reputation like yours—not entirely, anyway."

"Thanks for the vote of confidence."

Dillon looked at the plate in Clint's hand. It was mostly empty, showing the remnants of jambalaya and shrimp.

"How was the food?"

"As you said," Clint replied. "Excellent. I was just heading to the table for some gumbo."

"You'll love it," Dillon said. "By the way, you haven't seen Angela, have you?"

"Not in the past hour," Clint said. "Only when we first came on board." True, as far as it went.

"I suppose she'll show up as soon as she's hungry," he said.

"Tell me, are you and she involved?"

"We would be if I had my way," Dillon said, with a rueful grin. "So far, she's had hers."

"Which is?"

"To keep me at arm's length, I suppose," Dillon said. "She's been doin' a real good job of it."

"What about Ava?"

"Beautiful, isn't she?" Dillon asked. "And wait until you hear her sing."

"But you and she . . ."

"Oh, no," Dillon said. "She doesn't want that kind of a relationship with me, and I can't blame her. She works for me."

"Doesn't Angela?"

"Well, yes, but somehow that's different. Are you interested in Ava?"

"I think we're interested in each other," Clint said.

"Well then, my children," Dillon said, "I wish you luck. Go and enjoy . . . the gumbo, I mean."

Dillon walked away, laughing.

Angela showed up about an hour later. She was wearing a blue dress, and the first thing Clint noticed about it was a black smudge down at the bottom.

She was looking around the room, possibly seeking someone out, and it obviously wasn't Clint, because when she almost bumped into him she looked completely surprised.

"Oh, hey," she said. "Hi."

"Hello there," Clint said. "Your boss has been looking for you."

"Dean," she said, shaking her head. "I keep tryin' to let him down easy, but . . ."

"Don't worry about Dean," Clint said. "He falls in love all the time, and the ladies don't always fall back."

"Thanks," she said. "That makes me feel a lot better. I'm gonna get some food."

"What happened to your dress?"

"Huh? Whataya mean?"

He pointed and she looked down.

"Aw, damn," she said, "I must've brushed up against something on the dock. Ah well, I'm too hungry to go and change now."

She went off to get some food. Clint thought back to the two of them in his room. In his mind's eye he could see her undressing in front of him, and as hard as he tried he could not recall seeing that smudge there. She didn't get it on the dock; she got it someplace after she left his cabin.

THIRTEEN

That night was the first time Clint heard Ava sing.

After the champagne celebration he went back to his cabin and took a nap. The rocking of the boat seemed to lull him to sleep. But he wasn't too sleepy to be careful, though. There was a straight-backed wooden chair in the room and he stuck it under the door handle, just to double lock the door. Then he lay down with his gun nearby, hoping nobody would knock on his door.

Dean Dillon went back to his own cabin to change for the night. The tables would be going, and Ava would be singing. He'd check with the captain first, make sure everything up top was okay. He knew he was starting to bother the captain, though. The man scowled every time he saw Dillon coming, but goddamnit, he owned the boat. He had every right to go up to the bridge anytime he wanted to, no matter how annoyed Captain Hatton got.

He stuck his cut-down .45 into the shoulder rig underneath his jacket, then left the cabin.

Captain Jed Hatton wasn't at all sure he had done the right thing taking the job on this new boat, but how could he pass it up? After he'd piloted boats up and down the Mississippi for thirty years, somebody had finally come to him with an offer to be the captain of the largest boat ever to travel the river.

Well, this thing might have been big, but she was sluggish as hell. She was just too damn heavy! When it came time to correct the boat's trajectory, it was almost too late, so he had to start anticipating when it was time to maneuver. And he had to call on his knowledge of the river so as not to run her aground. There were shallow regions of the river other boats could still negotiate, but not this one. Too damn big, it'd run aground where most boats wouldn't.

And then there was the owner, Dean Dillon. The man was always coming up to the bridge to ask questions that didn't need to be asked. Was everything all right? "No, damnit, you built this boat too damn big."

Clint woke in two hours, got dressed, and headed for the main salon. The tables had all been moved, and now instead of holding trays of food, they held roulette wheels and faro layouts. Off to one side was a craps table. Dice was one game Clint had never gotten interested in.

All along the perimeter were tables with private

poker games going on, no house dealers. He saw King-dom at one table, and at another Troy Galvin, with Kathy standing behind him, her hands on his shoul-ders. And two other tables, as well.

He looked around for Dean Dillon, expecting to see him at a poker table, but instead he was leaning on the bar, keeping an eye on the room. Clint walked over to him.

"Buy you a drink?" Clint asked.

"I'll buy you one," Dillon said. "On the house. You're just in time."

"For what?"

"Ava's comin' out."

Before Ava, though, a man came out and sat at the piano. He played a few notes, and then Ava walked out, wearing a gown that showed her shoulders and a lot of her breasts. Her smooth, cocoa skin was flaw-less and went well with the maroon of her long gown. At every step, her thigh sneaked out through a slit in the gown.

She was magnificent.

"Can she really sing?" Clint asked.

"Like a bird," Dillon said. "She's not just beautiful, but it helps."

With the first note that came out of her mouth Clint knew Dillon was right. Ava had a beautiful voice. She drew the attention of everyone in the room, even the gamblers.

"Pretty smooth, huh?" Dillon asked

"She's great," Clint said.

"Yeah, she is, but I was talking about the boat. Pretty smooth ride, huh?"

"Real smooth," Clint said. "It put me to sleep for two hours."

"See how safe you feel? You fell asleep?"

"Actually, I did that to calm my nerves."

Dillon handed him a beer and said, "Aw, you're kiddin', Clint."

"Yeah, Dean," Clint said, "I'm kidding."

"Yeah, I knew it. Listen, I gotta go talk to the captain."

"Again? Doesn't that bother him?"

"Yeah, it does, but too bad. I own the damn boat."

"Is he an old-timer?"

"Yeah, he is. Why?"

"Those guys always figure the boat's theirs, no matter who owns it," Clint said. "Be careful. He might have you tossed over the side."

"Don't worry," Dillon said, "nobody's goin' over the side. Not on this trip."

THE PRESENT

Clint grabbed Angela's arm and said, "We have to go over the side."

FOURTEEN

ONE DAY EARLIER . . .

Two days out and everything seemed to be going along fine.

Dillon's passengers—many of them his guests—seemed to be enjoying themselves. Ava was very popular for her singing, as well as her beauty.

Kingdom was winning a lot of money at his table.

Galvin was winning at his table.

Kathy had not approached Kingdom again with her offer. He figured she had either changed her mind or had not been able to get away.

Clint had not been invited on board to play poker, so he had refrained from joining any of the table action. However, he had played blackjack at Angela's table a time or two. His opinion of her as a dealer was not high. In fact, she simply was not very good at it.

Ava and Clint had spent one night together, but last night she had not come to his cabin.

Also, Angela had not come back. Not yet, anyway.

Dillon was walking around the boat with his chest out, very happy with the way things had been going.

The Warrant brothers—Dillon's security force— were either very good at their job or very bad. Either way, Sam and Lou kept out of sight.

Dillon had taken Clint up to the bridge to meet the captain once. Clint recognized the man as soon as he entered the bridge. Not that he'd ever met him before, but Captain Hatton was exactly like other old-time riverboat captains Clint had met. He didn't like to have anyone on his bridge. Not even the owner of the boat.

"Captain, this is Clint Adams."

Hatton turned and looked at both Dillon and Clint.

"What's the Gunsmith doin' on my boat?" he demanded.

"He's my guest," Dean Dillon said, "and I'll remind you that this is my boat."

The captain compressed his lips in annoyance.

"All right," he said, "what's he doin' on my bridge?"

"I just brought him up to have a look," Dillon said. "And for the two of you to meet."

"Very well," the man said. "We've met. Now get off my bridge."

Hatton was a craggy-faced man who could have been fifty or seventy. Also on the bridge with him was his copilot, a man in his thirties. Clint looked at that man and received a helpless shrug in return.

"See here, Captain—" Dillon started.

"Never mind, Dean," Clint said. "It's okay. The captain has lots of work to do."

In point of fact, the captain looked worried to Clint. Something was on the man's mind.

"I think we should let him go back to it," Clint added.

"Yeah, fine," Dillon said. "Let's go back to the main salon."

Just outside the bridge they stopped and looked down at the water.

"It takes a lot of be a captain on this river," Clint said. "The depth changes so drastically from point to point. And the river changes."

"No reason for him to be that rude, though," Dillon said. "Maybe I'll replace him after we get back."

"I'd wait and see if he's a good captain first, if I was you," Clint said. "I'd much prefer to have a good captain than a polite one."

"You're probably right."

They started walking to the salon together.

"I saw you playing blackjack a couple of times at Angela's table. What do you think of her?"

"As a person I think she's lovely," Clint said.

"And as a blackjack dealer?"

"Not so good."

"What's wrong with her?"

"She doesn't handle the cards as well as she should," Clint said. "Doesn't make the correct plays when she should."

Dillon frowned. "Is she costing me money?"

Clint hesitated, then said, "Not a lot. I wouldn't let her handle a high-stakes table, though."

"Should I fire her?"

"Do you want to fire her?" Clint asked.

"Hell, no."

"Then don't," Clint said. "You're the boss."

"Yeah, I am," Dillon said.

They reached the salon and stopped at the main door.

"This looks like a success to me," Dillon said.

"And to me."

"You're not playing poker?"

"Not so far."

"What about tonight?"

Clint shrugged. "Maybe. First a drink."

"I'll join you," Dillon said. "Come on. To the bar."

FIFTEEN

"We can't jump from this deck," Clint said. "We have to work our way down."

"Do we have time?" Angela asked.

"I hope so," Clint said. "and I hope we can find the others. Dean, Ava . . ."

In the moonlight he could see people already in the water. Some of them were swimming, some weren't. Some were already just floating corpses.

"Where's the fire?" Angela asked.

"Seems to be belowdecks," Clint said, pointing. "Look, there . . . the flames are coming up from below."

"Clint," she said, "there's something belowdecks—"

"I know there is, Angela," he said, grabbing her arm. "It's fire."

He pulled her toward the stairway. He wanted to

get down to the first deck and then get the hell off the boat . . .

FOUR HOURS BEFORE . . .

Clint entered the salon that night intending to play some poker. He'd played a bit the night before, but not at either Kingdom or Galvin's table. He just had to decide which table to go to tonight.

As he had the other nights, he started at the bar. When he got there, Ava was already there, drinking a glass of champagne.

"Celebrating?" he asked.

"I just like champagne," she said. "What about you?"

"Beer," Clint said. "Usually beer."

He waved at the bartender, who knew by now to bring him a beer.

"Sorry I didn't come by last night?" she said.

"We didn't have a date or anything," he sad. "It's fine if you had something else to do."

"Actually, I rehearsed until late, so I was pretty tired," she said. "And I had to save my voice."

"Well," he said, raising his beer, "it's certainly worth saving."

"Thank you." She sipped her drink. "The champagne helps."

"That's good."

"Are you enjoying yourself?" she asked. "I mean, in general?"

"In general, I think if I had paid for this, I'd be disappointed."

"Why?"

"Um . . . well, don't tell Dean this, okay?"

"Okay."

"There's really nothing going on here that I couldn't see on dry land," he said, "and I'd rather be on dry land."

"You don't like riverboats?"

"I love riverboats."

"Ah," she said, "you don't like this riverboat."

"See why I don't want you to tell Dean?"

"What's wrong with it?" she asked, then added, "Just between you and me."

"Bigger isn't always better," he said.

"It's too big?"

"It's too damn big," he said, "and too damn heavy."

Suddenly, he wondered if that was what was bothering the captain, as well. Maybe the ship was just too big and heavy to maneuver safely and properly.

"But . . . according to Dean, that's the selling point," she said.

"Yeah," he said, "for Dean. He just always wants the biggest and the best, but ask the passengers. I mean, any passenger on any riverboat. They're not on it because it's the best, or the biggest. It's not about that."

"What's it about?"

"I think it's about the river," Clint said. "Passengers, crew, captain, I think they're all on a boat because they love the river."

"And do you love the river?"

"I do," he said. "It's unpredictable. Sort of like a woman—and you know how much I love women."

"Oh yes," she said, "you do love your women. Speaking of which, has little Angela thrown herself at you yet?"

"Why would you ask that?"

"Because I see the way she looks at you," she said. "Also, I think I wanted to see if you would be a gentleman—and you were."

"So I pass."

She raised her glass to him and said, "With flying colors, Clint Adams."

SIXTEEN

Clint played poker with Galvin that night. He watched as Kathy stood behind the man, keeping her hands on his shoulders as if for moral support. He wondered if Galvin could play without Kathy there.

And then he noticed something. It was the way Kathy was looking at him from hand to hand. He wondered what was going on, and then he got it. She was signaling him. She was trying to let him know when Galvin had a strong hand, and when he had a weak hand.

But why? he wondered. What was going on? Trouble in paradise? And was this her way of getting back at her man? By giving up his hands?

Cheating was a very simple thing. You really didn't have to know exactly what your opponent had. What you needed was just a hint of whether he was strong or weak, and that seemed to be what she was trying to give Clint.

Only he didn't want it. If and when he beat somebody at poker, he wanted it to be on the up-and-up.
He didn't need any help beating other players. He
was that confident in his abilities.

So after a while he just stopped looking at Kathy.

From across the room Kingdom was watching Galvin
and Clint. He was also watching Kathy. It looked to
him like she was sending signals. He wondered if she
had made the same offer to Clint Adams that she had
made to him, and if Adams had taken her up on it. He
didn't see why someone like Adams would need or
want that kind of advantage.

There were seats available at both tables, both his
and theirs. He wondered how long it would take for
him and Adams to end up at the same table together.

Dillon watched the proceedings from the bar, listened
to Ava sing, watched Angela deal. He guessed that he
was so interested in Angela that he hadn't noticed
that she wasn't very good at her job. He wondered if
he'd made the same mistake with the captain. When
they got back to New Orleans, he'd have to take stock,
decide what he wanted to do.

Maybe he should give Angela the rest of the night
off.

Angela was dealing and saw Dillon looking over at
her. She looked over at Clint playing poker and not
paying her any mind. Then she looked at Ava, up on
the stage singing, with the piano player next to her.
Bitch. That dark hair and dark skin, it was all over

New Orleans. She, Angela, was the one who was unusual. She was the one who should have been considered exotic.

She turned her head and saw Dillon walking across the floor to her.

"Hey, sweetie, I need a card," one of the players said. "You fallin' asleep there?"

"Sorry," she said, and dealt him the card he needed for twenty-one.

"Yes!" he said.

Dillon wasn't alone. He had one of the male dealers with him. Had he finally figured out that she was bad at this?

"Okay, honey," he said to her, "why don't you take the rest of the night off?"

"And do what?" she asked, wondering what the catch was.

"Why don't you just relax?" he asked her.

She put the cards down. "Fine with me."

She got out from behind the table and allowed the male dealer to move into her spot.

"Thank God," one of the players said. "I hope you at least know what you're doin', son."

"Don't worry, my friend," Dillon said.

As Angela walked away, she heard the player say, "Send her to my room, if you want, but don't let her deal anymore."

Dillon laughed, the bastard.

She crossed the room to Clint's table, moved up behind him, and bent over, pressing her lips to his ear.

"I have the rest of the night off," she said. "Come to my cabin."

He looked up at her and smiled, but before he could say yes or no, she walked away.

He looked at the cards in his hand. Three kings. He made a point of not looking at Kathy, but it was becoming harder and harder.

"I call," Galvin said, calling Clint's bet. "Three sevens."

Clint put his cards down, raked in his pot, and said, "I think that's it for me, gents."

"You leavin' already?" Galvin asked. "We just got started."

"There'll be other nights, Mr. Galvin," Clint said.

He pocketed his money and stood up. Before he played with Galvin again, he'd have to have a heart-to-heart with Kathy—if he could separate the two.

He knocked on Angela's door.

"Did I take you away from something important?" she asked when she opened it. "A winning streak, maybe?"

"Winning, yes," he said, "but nothing really important."

She backed away to allow him to enter.

"Dean gave me the rest of the night off," she told him.

"So you told me. Any idea why?"

"I don't know," she said. "Maybe he thought I'd spend the time with him, but I'd much rather spend it with you."

"Angela, Dean's my friend," Clint said. "I don't want to get in between you two—"

"There's nothin' goin' on between me and Dean,

Clint," she said. "He may want to, but I don't, and I made that decision before I ever met you."

She moved closer to him and put her hands on his chest.

"We have more time now than we did the first day," she said, playing with a button on his shirt. "I'd like to go nice and slow this time."

"Sounds good to me—" he started, but that was when they heard the noise. It was a great big *Whump!* that they felt in the floor.

"What the hell was that?" he asked.

SEVENTEEN

When they got to the deck, they saw people running back and forth and, beneath them, the flames. And the boat started to list to one side . . .

They were going down!

Still holding tightly to Angela's arm, Clint practically dragged her down the stairs to the next deck. The crush of people kept them from getting to the first deck, however.

"Angela, do you have any idea how many people this boat holds?"

"I think I heard Dean saying he could get eighteen hundred on board."

"And how many for this cruise?"

"Not a full load," she said, "but there still has to be eight or nine hundred."

And they were all trying to get to safety as the flames started to spread.

Clint looked around. There was no way he could

find Dean or Ava in this crush of humanity. The boat
listed even more to the left, and they had to hold on
so they wouldn't be thrown off balance.

"We should get to the other side if we're gonna
jump off," she said. "That side is lower."

"No, the boat's listing that way," he said. "If we
jump off that side the boat might roll. Anybody in the
water then will be crushed. We've got to go over on
this side. If it rolls, I want to be on the other side of it."

He wondered where the captain was. If the man
was good at his job, he was still on the bridge.

Captain Hatton gritted his teeth as he held onto the
wheel of the big riverboat. This damn boat . . .

He knew that this was not his fault. He hadn't hit
anything. The fault was with the boat itself, and when
he saw the flames he was convinced that the problem
came from belowdecks. He'd felt the explosion beneath his feet and knew immediately what it was.

The boat continued to list to the port side, no matter
how he tried to fight it. It was his guess they were taking on water on that side.

He maintained as much forward motion as he could.
There was just the slightest chance he could reach a
bend in the river where the water was shallow. It could
save the boat from going completely under.

Goddamn weight of the damn vessel!

Dean Dillon felt the deck shudder beneath his feet and
knew something was wrong.

The rest of the people in the salon all stopped what
they were doing and froze. Cards, dice, the roulette

wheel—they all stopped. The piano ceased to play and Ava stopped singing.

"What was that?" one person yelled.

Dillon knew he had to do something quickly, so he left the bar and hurried to get up on the stage with Ava.

"Ladies and gentlemen," he said, "everythin' is under control, I assure you. Just go on with your gambling, enjoy the music. This boat is quite safe. I'm sure there's a logical explanation—"

Abruptly, the boat listed to port, and Dillon was almost thrown off balance. Some glasses hit the deck and shattered, and the piano rolled on its rollers.

"We're sinking!" somebody shouted, and that was it.

Everyone panicked and ran for the doors.

Dillon reached out, grabbed Ava's arm, and said, "Come on!"

THE PRESENT . . .

Clint and Angela were flattened against a wall on the second deck as people ran by. The majority of the passengers did not seem to have grasped the gravity of the situation yet. They were still running to and fro rather than abandoning ship. People were being knocked off their feet and trampled.

Clint helped an older woman to her feet before she got trampled, and he said to her, "You have to jump overboard."

She stared at him as if he was crazy, then shook loose and started running.

"You can't help everyone, Clint," Angela said. "We have to save ourselves."

"All right," he said. "Let's get off this thing."

They had to push through a wave of people in order to get to the rail.

"Can you swim?" he asked her.

"I don't know," she said honestly. "I guess we're about to find out."

EIGHTEEN

When they hit the water, it was ice cold. The shock went right through Clint, but he knew he had to keep hold of Angela. Otherwise, if she couldn't swim, she was finished.

The force with which they struck the water took them under immediately. Angela started to thrash, almost pulling free of his hold. He grabbed her around the waist so he'd be sure not to lose her, and kicked for the surface. But she was struggling so much she was keeping them under. There was a chance she could drown them both. If that was the case, he'd have to let her go or die with her.

He shook her, trying to send her a message to relax and let him do the work. Finally, she seemed to get the message. Her struggles ceased and he was able to carry them both to the surface.

Their heads broke the surface and he took a deep breath. He looked over at her and saw the reason she had stopped struggling. She was unconscious. She had probably swallowed a lot of water.

"Angela!" he called. "Angela! You have to wake up."

His arm was around her waist, so he squeezed, trying to drive water out of her lungs. He did it again and again, and finally her mouth opened and water came streaming out. She choked, and he tried to keep her chin above water, so she didn't just take more in.

She choked again, her eyes fluttered, and she looked directly at him, which was a very good sign.

"What happened?" she asked.

"You're all right," he said. "You swallowed some water and lost consciousness for a few minutes."

She looked around, then turned and looked up at the burning boat.

"Oh my God," she said, as it all came back to her. "Dean's perfect boat."

"Yeah."

Something hit the water to their right, and then to their left.

"What's happening?" she asked.

"People are getting the message," he said. "They're jumping off."

But it was only a smattering of people. He was afraid the majority of them were jumping off the left side, seeing that it was not as high a jump.

If the boat rolled, they'd all be crushed.

Dean Dillon could not believe his eyes. His perfect riverboat was on fire, and sinking. That goddamn captain, he thought, he must've hit something.

He had Ava by the arm, pulling her along as she panicked.

"We're gonna die!" she told him.

"We're not gonna die, Ava," he said. "We gonna get off."

Although what he was thinking was that he should probably die. Go down with the ship, because after this he was finished. His investors would be after him, and there'd be a thousand lawsuits.

No, he was going to stay alive, if only to get his hands around that captain's throat.

"Come on, Ava," he said. "we've got to get off this boat."

"How?"

"We're gonna jump overboard."

She grabbed his arm with both hands and said, "I can't swim!"

"Don't worry," he said. "Just hold onto me."

The Warrant brothers had no idea what had happened. They were supposed to be on duty, but they were in their cabin, sharing a little red-haired girl who worked in the kitchen. They often shared a girl between them. The trick was finding a girl who didn't mind, didn't find it odd.

The girl from the kitchen not only didn't mind it, she was excited by it.

"I ain't never been with two boys at one time," she'd said.

"It'll be somethin' new for you," Sam had said, and she agreed.

So they were on the bed, Sam's penis in the girl's mouth while Lou fucked her from behind, and when the boat listed to port the first time, they were all thrown off and to the floor.

"What the hell was that?" the girl demanded. She'd just barely avoided biting Sam as his dick slid from her mouth. From behind, Lou was still inside of her.

"I dunno," Sam said.

"Damn!" Lou said. "We gotta find out."

They all got dressed quickly and left the cabin. When they got to the deck, panic had already set in, and they could see the flames.

"Are we sinkin'?" the girl asked.

"Looks like it," Sam said.

"This boat ain't supposed to be able to sink," Lou reminded his brother.

Sam took the girl by the shoulders and said, "You gotta get off this boat."

"What about you two?" she asked.

"We're security," Sam said. "We gotta see to people."

"You're so brave," she said. She kissed them both quickly and ran off into the crowd.

"We gotta see to people?" Lou asked. "We gotta get off this boat."

"You think this is our fault?" Sam asked. "'cause we wuz havin' sex instead of doin' our job?"

"Well, yeah, it could be," Lou said. "What's the damn difference? Everybody's gotta get off this boat."

"What if we run into Mr. Dillon?" Sam asked.

"Well, then that would mean we wuz all still alive, Sam," Lou said. "We can worry about the rest of it later. For now, let's just stay alive."

"Okay," his brother said, "that sounds like a good plan."

NINETEEN

"What do we do now?" Angela asked.

"We swim for shore."

"Which way?"

It was dark. Clint looked around, trying to find some lights that would indicate where shore was.

"I think we're simply going to have to swim away from the boat."

"What if we're goin' the wrong way?" she asked. "What if the other shore is closer?"

"We can't swim around the boat," he said. "It's too big."

Something floated near Angela and touched her. She turned and looked into the face of a dead man.

"Jesus!" she said, pushing the body away from her.

There were no marks on the man. He hadn't been burned, he had apparently drowned.

"Come on, Angela," Clint said. "We've got to get started before this cold water gets to us."

"Aren't there supposed to be lifeboats?" she asked him.

"Yes," he said, "and somebody should be seeing to it that they're lowered—the Warrant brothers, or Dean himself. Or whatever crewmen are charged with that job. Maybe they did. Maybe the boats are in the water on the other side. Let's hope so, because that would save quite a few lives."

"I'm so c-cold," Angela said, her teeth chattering.

"I know, that's why we have to start swimming. It'll warm us up."

She looked around in vain for a boat.

"Where are the lifeboats?" Ava asked.

"No time," Dillon said. "You'll have to jump."

"What about you?"

"I am gonna see what's happening with the life-boats," he said.

"I'll go with you."

"Ava—"

"I told you, I can't swim, and if you're not gonna jump with me, I'll drown."

"All right," he said. "All right. Come with me. If we can't find out what's going on, we'll jump."

"Okay," she agreed.

"Are the lifeboats away?" the captain asked one of his crewmen.

"No, sir."

"Why not?"

"Too much panic, Captain," the man said.

"Among the passengers?"

"And crew."

The captain had brought only two crew members with him when he took the job, his copilot and this crewman. The other crew members had been hired by Dean Dillon.

"Goddamnit!" he growled.

"What are we going to do, Captain?" the copilot asked.

"We're in the shallows," the captain said. "Deep enough for people to swim, but not deep enough for the boat to sink completely. We should be all right, as long as the boat doesn't flip."

The copilot and crewman exchanged a look. They knew that the captain had saved the *Dolly Madison* from being a total loss. But would the owner see it that way?

They had swum only a hundred yards or so when suddenly Clint felt something beneath his feet. The bottom?

"Is that the bottom?" Angela asked.

They went a few more yards and then were able to stand.

"Are we on shore?" she asked.

"No," he said, "it's just shallow here."

They turned and looked at the *Dolly Madison*.

"What's happening?" Angela asked.

"It's righting itself," he said.

The boat, which had listed so far to the left, had started to come back to the right.

"It's not sinkin'?" she asked.

"It is," Clint said. "Look, the first deck is underwater, but it's not sinking completely. It's going to sit on the shallow bottom."

"Then it's safe?" she asked. "We didn't have to jump, after all?"

"It's far from safe," Clint said. "It's still burning." He took her arm. "Come on, we still have to get to shore."

But they were able to wade the rest of the way.

TWENTY

As the boat began to list back to the starboard side, Ava grabbed Dillon and asked, "What's happening?"

"We're straightening out," he said.

They were on the second deck, looking down. Dillon could see that trying to get to the lifeboats was futile. The first deck was underwater. At least that would extinguish the fire—but then he saw that the flames had leaped to the second deck. The source of the fire was underwater, but the flames were still traveling.

"Where's the damn crew?" he said, aloud. "Why aren't they fighting the fire, helping the passengers?"

"Where are Sam and Lou?" she asked.

"If I find those two, I'll kill 'em," Dillon said.

"Dean, what do we do?"

He turned and looked at her. "What we were going to do in the first place," he said. "We have to abandon ship."

She clutched him and said, "You won't let me drown?"

"I promise, Ava," he said. "I won't let you drown."

"Captain," the copilot said, "she's settled on the bottom."

"She's not gonna sink, Captain," the crewman said, "but she's still burnin'."

"A good crew would be seein' to that," the captain complained. "When I find that Dillon, I'm gonna kill him."

"If he's still alive," the copilot said.

"He better be alive!" the captain said. "So I can get my hands on him." He turned and looked at his two men. "All right, lads, over the side with ya."

"What about you, Captain?" the crewman asked.

"I'm the captain," he said simply.

"I know you gotta go down with the ship, Captain," the copilot said, "but it's down. It ain't sinkin' anymore. You saved it."

"Yeah," Captain Hatton said, "I saved it so it could burn."

"That ain't your fault," the crewman said.

"Actually, it is," the captain said. "I should've insisted on hirin' the whole crew myself. We got an inexperienced owner, an inexperienced crew, and look what happened."

"What did happen, Captain?" the copilot asked.

"Near as I can figure," Hatton said, "there must've been an explosion belowdecks. Might've blown a hole in the port side. We took on water there, started listin' to that side. If we hadn't got to the shallows, this tub would've flipped."

"So the question is, what caused the explosion?" the copilot said.

"There'll be an investigation," the captain said. "I'll see to it. Now, both of you, over the starboard side. Get yerselves to shore."

"Captain," the copilot said, "you don't gotta burn up with the ship—"

"I know that," Hatton said. "Don't worry, I'll be along. But I'll be the last one off. At least I can do my job to that degree. Now git, both of you."

"Captain—" the crewman started.

"Cap—" the copilot tried.

"That's an order, lads!" Captain Hatton said. "Off with yer."

The two men exchanged a glance, then slowly left the bridge and made their way to the rail. The captain watched them go over the side. Satisfied that they were safe in the water, he turned his attention to the fire.

TWENTY-ONE

When Clint and Angela reached the shore, Clint literally carried her to dry ground, where they both collapsed, breathing heavily.

"Are you all right?" he asked her.

"Yes . . . I think . . . so," she panted. "Just . . . can't . . . talk . . ."

"Okay, relax," he told her. "Catch your breath."

With all the people who were on the *Dolly Madison*, there had to be a lot of them reaching shore on either side. If the other shore was farther, maybe fewer people would make it there, but if it was as shallow there as on this side, Clint figured there should be a lot of survivors. He figured this in spite of the fact that he and Angela had seen many dead bodies floating in the river.

He considered walking up and down the shore looking for survivors, but what could he do for them? He might be better off staying where he was with

Angela, catching his breath, and then walking inland
to see where they were. He didn't know if they were
near a town, but maybe they could find their way to a
house, where people could help them.

He wondered about Ava, and Dillon. Also about the
captain. Was he bound and determined to go down
with the ship?

And what the hell had happened? What was that
sound, and the vibration beneath their feet? All he could
figure was that there had been an explosion. Could one
of the steam engines have exploded? Would that blow a
hole in the side of the boat? And start a fire?

"What are you thinkin'?" Angela asked, sounding
like she'd gotten her breath back.

"Trying to figure what happened," Clint said. "It
had to be some kind accident . . . unless Dillon has
some enemies I don't know about."

"Sabotage?"

Clint shrugged. "Maybe somebody didn't want
Dean to have the biggest boat on the Mississippi."

"But . . . who?" she asked. "Couldn't the captain
have just run it aground? Or hit something?"

"And started a fire? I doubt it."

Angela looked out at the water, where the *Dolly
Madison* was just sitting, her first deck underwater, the
other two decks still showing flames.

"I wonder where Dean is," she said. "And what
about the cargo?"

"Cargo?"

"All that stuff that was being shipped upriver," she
said.

"Like what?" Clint asked. "Anything important?"

She hesitated, then shrugged and said, "I don't know. I wasn't around when Dean was making arrangements. I don't even know if he's aware of what was being shipped." She looked at Clint. "If somebody was shipping somethin' valuable, why would they say so?"

"I saw plenty of crates being loaded on," Clint said. "I wish I could talk to the captain. He'd probably know what happened. He could say whether it was an accident or not."

"Would he admit it if he ran into somethin'?" she asked.

"I don't know," Clint said. "I only met him briefly. He was crotchety, but I had the impression he knew what he was doing."

"That fire is still burnin'," she said.

"That's something else I'm wondering about," Clint said. "The fire. Why isn't the crew battling it?"

"They all went overboard, I guess."

"Did Dean hire the crew? Or did the captain?"

"Dean," she said. "I know that for a fact. I think the captain brought a couple of men with him, but the rest were hired by Dean."

"I wonder if he tried to save money on a crew?" Clint said.

"With all the money he spent on the boat itself?" she asked.

Clint looked at her.

"Did he dicker with you on your pay?"

"Well . . . yes."

"He probably did that with everyone," Clint said. "Dealers, crew, stevedores, Ava . . . Damnit, Dean."

"He sabotaged himself?"

"In a way," Clint said. "If he scrimped on the crew, then they simply weren't good enough to fight the fire. With an experienced crew, that boat wouldn't be burning right now. She'd be salvageable."

"Dean always said that the boat couldn't sink, and would never burn. Supposedly, the wood was treated with something special to keep it from burning."

"Well, either it wasn't treated well enough," Clint said, "or . . ."

"Or what?"

"He may have been talking about the boat not burning under normal circumstances."

"Which this isn't?" she asked.

"We don't know," Clint said. "If somebody set the fire, and used some kind of oil . . ."

They both stared out at the boat, and Clint noticed that it was mostly burning up front, not the middle or the back.

"If the fire was set in the front, then that's what's burning," he said. "It's not spreading to the rest of the boat because of the special wood treatment."

"If that's true, then somebody must have set it. Someone who knew that," she said. "But who?"

"That's something Dean and his investors are going to have to find out," Clint said. "Right now we have to do something about getting dry."

"How are we gonna do that?"

"We'll have to start a fire," Clint said. "Come, help me gather some wood."

"What do you have to start a fire with?" she asked. "Any matches you have will be wet."

"I've started plenty of fires in my time without matches," he told her.

TWENTY-TWO

They found a clearing, the right kind of wood, and the right kind of stones so that Clint could cause a spark and start a fire. They sat close to it so the heat would dry their clothes.

Something that surprised Clint was that he had gotten out of the water without losing his gun. Wearing it was so second nature to him that it had never occurred to him to unstrap it in the river and let it sink to the bottom so it wouldn't weigh him down. He just never noticed that it was any kind of a hindrance.

Staring out at the boat, he noticed for the first time that some of the flames he saw were not coming from it. They were coming from the opposite shore.

"Looks like some people made it to the other shore and had the same idea," he said.

"Where are we?" Angela asked. "How many miles did we cover?"

"I can't tell you that," Clint said. "I know the Mississippi winds through Louisiana for a long time. It doesn't even really start heading north until it crosses into Mississippi. And we were going upstream, which means we were covering ground much slower than we would if we were going downstream. We may be at Baton Rouge, or we may have gone as far as Vicksburg. To tell you the truth, I wasn't really paying that much attention."

He looked across the river again.

"It only seems to be a few hundred yards wide here, and not that deep. I know there are some places where the river is a mile wide and a couple of feet deep. We don't seem to be anywhere near that here. We're just going to have to wait and see, Angela."

He was cleaning his gun, getting it dry, when they heard some sounds in the brush. He stood up, gun in hand, as several people came into the light.

"Oh my God," a woman said. "We saw your light . . ."

Clint rushed forward to catch the middle-aged woman before she could fall. There were other people with her, men and women, about eleven altogether.

"We've been wanderin'," a man said, "and saw your fire . . ."

"Come and sit," Angela said. "Everyone."

"Have you seen any others?" Clint asked.

"Some," the woman said. "Some were going in the opposite direction, looking for help. We saw some . . . some bodies that washed up on shore." She started to cry. "What a horrible night."

Clint collected more wood so he could start a second fire. That way they'd all be able to sit close to the flames and dry out.

Pretty soon others arrived who had seen the two fires, and Clint started even more. Eventually they had about six campfires going, and more than forty people sitting around them.

"Does anybody know where we are?" someone asked.

"I think we're around St. Louis," someone said, hopefully.

"No," another voice argued, "we haven't come nearly that far."

"There's really no point in guessing," Clint said. "At first light we can start walking and see where we end up."

"Shouldn't we stay here so we can be found?" a woman asked.

"By who?" another voice asked.

"Rescuers."

"You know how long it'll take before someone comes looking for us?"

People started to argue loudly, and Clint decided to let them go. Let them tire themselves out even more, he figured, and eventually they did. Before long they were all sitting around the fire with their heads lolling forward or back. Some of them simply used each other to lean against or lie on. Angela was sitting with her head on Clint's shoulder.

With all the people who had come into their camp, they still had not seen either Dean Dillon or Ava—or the Warrant brothers. Clint wanted to talk to those two!

"Maybe," Angela said to him, "some of us should stay here while others go searching for help."

"The women can stay behind," Clint said. "When we find out where we are, or what town we're near, we can come back with help."

"I don't want to stay here with a bunch of hysterical women," she said.

"Let's discuss it when the sun comes up," he said.

It was spring, but still cold along the shores of the Mississippi at night. They huddled together and kept the fire high for warmth.

Clint wondered about the people across the river, on the other shore. Was Dillon there with Ava? Was the captain there? He looked at the people around him. They all seemed to be passengers, no crew. Had the crew all swum to the other side?

As the sun came up, Clint wished for some coffee. Angela was sound asleep, and he felt bad, but he had to nudge her awake.

"Come on," he said, "time to start walking."

She sat up, rubbing her face and her eyes as he stood up.

"Where are you going?" one woman asked.

"What's happenin'?" another said.

"Folks, I'm going to start walking inland to see if I can figure out where we are. Anyone who wants to come along is welcome. I was thinking that the women could stay here and wait for us to come back with help."

"What if you don't come back?" a woman asked.

"We'll freeze to death," another added.

"The sun will warm you soon enough," Clint said. "And we certainly will come back with help. We're not going to leave you stranded here. At least, I'm not."

"I'll go along," a young man said.

"Me, too," an older man said.

"Jerry, you have to stay with me," his wife said, grabbing his arm.

He leaned over, patted her hand, and spoke to her in a low, soothing voice. She nodded, and released his arm, seeming to be appeased, but not happy.

"I'm coming," the man said.

In turn, six more men volunteered to go along, so Clint and eight other men ended up leaving camp to look for help.

"I'd like to come," Angela told Clint, "but I think I hurt my foot last night. I better stay behind."

"Okay," Clint said. "I'll be back as soon as I can with help."

She nodded, then stared out at the boat, which had stopped burning. The look on her face was one of longing, he thought, but he had no time to wonder about it. The boat was grounded, though, no question about that, the hold and the first deck filled with water.

"Okay, gents," Clint said, "let's get a move on. Maybe we can get back before nightfall."

TWENTY-THREE

They walked a couple of hours and came to a road, but it was forked.

"Which way?" someone asked.

"Both," Clint said. "We'll split up. Four can go that way, five this way. I'm going here." He pointed. "The rest of you decide who's going where."

It took them a while, with lots of arguing and cursing, but finally four of them joined Clint, while the other four followed the road the opposite way.

"Now I wish I had some of that river water on me," one of the men said after they'd walked another hour. "That sun is hot."

"We shoulda stayed by the river," another man said.

Clint ignored them. He hadn't even felt the need to learn the names of these men. He didn't expect to see any of them again after this was over.

The only man who seemed to walk without complaining—even when there were nine of them walking together—was the older man who had spoken softly to his wife.

"This is quite an adventure," he said to Clint.

"No one else seems to think so," Clint said.

"Well, why not?" the man asked. "We're all still alive, and I've never gone through anything like this before."

Clint looked at the man and was surprised to see that he actually looked happy. The only thing he could figure was that the man was happy to be away from his wife for a period of time.

"You're in pretty good shape," Clint said. "Younger men are lagging behind."

"I've worked hard for many years," the man said. "My name is Jerry, by the way."

"Clint."

The two men shook hands.

"You seem to have some leadership qualities, Clint," Jerry said. "Kept everybody together last night, even calm."

"There's no point in panicking, Jerry," Clint said. "Won't get anything accomplished that way."

"I couldn't agree more," Jerry said. "So, where do you think we're gonna end up?"

"Beats me," Clint said. "I just hope it's a big enough town to be able to help us all."

They walked a bit farther and then Jerry asked, "How did you manage to hold onto that gun while you were in the water?"

"It's like my arm," Clint said. "Someone would have had to tear it off."

He was sorry, though, that his Colt New Line, his little backup gun, was on the *Dolly Madison*. Luckily, the boat hadn't sunk completely, so when a salvage team was sent out to it maybe he could recover the gun. It had saved his life countless times.

From behind them they heard two people shout. When they turned, they saw three men on the ground.

"We can't walk anymore," one of them said.

Clint and Jerry put their hands on their hips and looked at them.

"Soft living," Jerry said.

"Definitely."

They walked back to where the men were sprawled on the ground.

"We're going to go on ahead and try to get help," Clint said to them. "Rest for a while, and when you feel better, start walking again."

"Wait, wait . . ." one of them said, gasping. He was in his thirties and certainly looked as if he should have been able to walk. "You have the only gun."

"That's right."

"What if there's Indians out here?" another asked.

Clint looked at Jerry, who said, "Easterner, here to see the Wild West from the safety of a riverboat."

Clint rolled his eyes.

"There are no Indians here," he said. "You'll be safe." He hesitated, then added, "However, there are some animals. Predators. But you should be safe as long as you start moving again."

He and Jerry started walking.

"Wait!" someone shouted.

"Animals?" another one called.

Jerry said, "That was mean."

Clint said, "Yeah."

To their credit the men tried to follow, but eventually Clint and Jerry outdistanced them.

"You know," Jerry said, "I've been thinking."

"About what?"

"I studied the route when we booked passage on the boat," he said. "I'm an engineer."

"What did you think of the boat?" Clint asked.

"In theory, it was a fascinating undertaking. But it didn't seem practical to me."

"Too heavy?" Clint asked.

"Too big and too heavy. I can't imagine the captain didn't have trouble trying to maneuver all the twists and turns of the river. Also, the day of the riverboat is gone. It wasn't a sound investment for anyone."

"That's Dean Dillon's specialty," Clint said. "Convincing people with money to invest in something that's not a sound investment."

"I see. You know him?"

"We're friends," Clint said, "sort of. What did you mean when you said you studied the route?"

"Well, by trying to figure the speed of the currents, and the speed that the boat was moving, I'm guessing that we're probably somewhere around Vicksburg."

"That would be helpful," Clint said. "That's a big city. We'd be able to get all the help we need, and someone to salvage the boat."

"I'm guessing, mind you," Jerry said.

"I think your guess is pretty damn good, Jerry."

"What makes you say that?"

Clint stopped walking and pointed. "That sign."

Jerry looked at the signpost and nodded. It said: "VICKSBURG, 3 miles."

TWENTY-FOUR

As they entered Vicksburg, Clint wasn't sure where they should go, so he decided the best thing would be to approach the law. They were attracting attention because of their condition, and Clint stopped one man and asked directions to the sheriff's office.

"Ain't got no sheriff," the man said, "but we got us a police station."

"That'll do," Clint said.

They followed the man's directions and found the station. They entered, and Clint asked for the chief of police. A portly man in his fifties said he was Chief Radcliffe. Clint and Jerry explained what had happened, and the chief didn't waste any time. He assured them rescue efforts would be mounted within the hour. He sent several of his men out to make arrangements.

"And go over to Anchor Line," he told one of the men. "We're gonna need their help."

"What's Anchor Line?" Jerry asked.

"They run a riverboat out of here called the *City of Vicksburg*," Radcliffe said. "They also have some flat-boats we're gonna need."

Clint took the time to explain fully the situation he and Jerry had left behind them: the boat sitting in shallow water, still burning when they left; survivors on both shores, the Mississippi side and the Louisiana side.

"I'll send some telegrams, see if we can't get some help from Louisiana," the chief said.

The door opened then, and a tall, barrel-chested fellow in his fifties entered, black hair shot with gray.

"Mr. Adams, this is Fred Ward," Radcliffe said. "He manages Anchor Line and is in charge of all their boats. Fred, Clint Adams and Jerry . . ."

"Sumner," Jerry said. It was the first time Clint had heard his last name.

"Mr. Sumner."

"Gents," Ward said. "Every boat we have is at your disposal."

"I'm sure Dean Dillon will appreciate your help, Mr. Ward," Clint said.

"I hope so," Ward said.

"Why wouldn't he?"

"Dillon came to us with his plans for the *Dolly Madison*," the man explained. "We turned him down."

"Why?" Jerry asked.

"Well, aside from the fact that we didn't want to run another riverboat on the Mississippi," Ward said, "I told him his boat would be too big, and too heavy. A recipe for disaster. I guess I was right."

"That may not be what the problem was, Mr. Ward," Clint said. "You see, there was an explosion on board."

"Well, I guess we won't know for sure until my men get out there."

Clint turned to the chief.

"I want to go along," he said.

"Me, too," Jerry said.

"Are you sure you're up to it?" Radcliffe asked. "You men need some rest."

"There are a bunch of people out there who I gave my promise to, Chief," Clint said. "I told them I was coming back with help, and that's what I intend to do."

"And my wife is one of them," Jerry said.

"Well, it's all right with me if it's okay with Fred," the chief said.

They all looked at Ward. He and the chief were about the same age, and Clint sensed a friendship there.

"It's okay with me," Ward said. "You better get down to the dock. My men are ready to go."

"Some of my men will go along, as well," the chief said. "Good luck."

Clint and Jerry left the police station and, with six police officers, headed to the docks.

There were two flat-bottom boats loaded and ready to go. They had to use them because even though Clint explained how deep the *Dolly Madison* was sitting, there was still no way for them to know what kind of shallows they'd be dealing with. They could be as little as three feet.

Running with the current, they made good time to

the bend in the river where the *Dolly Madison* had stalled. Still, it took hours to get there and it was past midday when they arrived.

The rescue operation was being run by a man named Stan McKay. Clint was on the same boat with him and three policemen, while Jerry was on the other boat with three policemen. Jerry's boat made its way toward the Mississippi shore, where he and Clint had left Jerry's wife and the others. Jerry and the policemen disembarked, waded ashore, and headed inland to find them.

Clint's boat pulled up alongside the *Dolly Madison*.

"We better check and see if there are any survivors on board," McKay reasoned.

They boarded the boat, and even though her first deck was underwater, it was only up to their shins and they were able to walk.

"Let's check the bridge," McKay said.

He, Clint, and the policemen used the stairs to get to the third deck and approach the wheelhouse. As McKay opened the door, Captain Hatton looked up from his seated position and said, "Well what the hell took ya so long?"

TWENTY-FIVE

Captain Hatton had recognized the fact that the *Dolly Madison* was not going to sink. In fact, he had done everything he could to get the boat to that bend in the river near Vicksburg, as he knew the water was shallow there.

"Dillon's going to be happy that you saved his boat," Stan McKay said.

"Fool made the boat too big and too heavy," Hatton said.

"Seems like everybody has that opinion except for him," Clint said.

"What about the fire?" McKay asked Hatton. "Any idea what started that?"

"I ain't been down there, but it had to be an explosion."

"I agree," Clint said. "I could feel it through the deck beneath my feet."

"I'll take some of my men down there and have a look," McKay said. "Meanwhile, I'll send my boat across the river to pick up some people and take them to Vicksburg."

"You did a good job, Captain," Clint said, shaking the man's hand. "I'll be telling Dean Dillon that."

"I don't think that'll make much of a difference," Hatton said.

"Why do you say that?"

"That friend of yours is gonna be lookin' for somebody to blame," the captain said. "He ain't about to take the blame himself."

Clint was afraid the captain had Dean Dillon pegged right.

There was nobody else on board. McKay had to have a couple of his men swim underwater to see what the damage was in the hold of the boat. They both came up shaking their heads.

"There's a hole in the boat on the port side," one of them said. "Looks like it was blown out."

"What caused the explosion?" Clint asked.

"If you ask me," the man said, "somebody put some dynamite down there."

"Sabotage?" McKay asked.

The man said, "Looks like it to me," and his partner nodded his agreement.

Clint looked at the captain, who had accompanied them down to the first deck.

"Dillon can't blame this on you," he said.

Hatton laughed and said, "Watch him."

Captain Hatton came aboard their flatboat and then Clint and McKay went over to the Louisiana shore to pick up some survivors. They didn't all fit on the two boats, so on the Mississippi side they made arrangements for some wagons to pick people up, as well.

It was nightfall when Clint got into a hotel in Vicksburg, was able to take a bath, change his clothes, and get a hot meal. He'd been able to salvage his belongings from the *Dolly Madison*, including his beloved Colt New Line.

Shelters had been set up for a lot of the survivors who could not afford to get themselves hotel rooms. Many of them had lost their money along the way, or had left it on the boat and had not been able to recover it yet. Arrangements were being made for a salvage run the next day.

Angela had been able to get a room at the same hotel as Clint. Ava had been recovered from the Louisiana side, and it turned out she had some family in Vicksburg, so she was staying with them.

The Warrant brothers had not turned up. The bodies that had washed up onto the shores had not yet been collected. That would be done last, after the living were seen to.

Dean Dillon was nowhere to be found.

Clint actually had a meal with Jerry Sumner that night. Jerry's wife was in a hotel room, in bed wrapped in a blanket. They were staying in the same hotel as Clint, and they had their meal in the hotel dining room.

"She won't come out," he told Clint.

"You can't really blame her," Clint said. "She's been through an ordeal."

"What's on your agenda for tomorrow?" Jerry asked.

"I was thinking about going out to the boat again with McKay and his men. Dean Dillon is still among the missing. What about you?"

"I offered to go out and look at the boat as an engineer. Maybe I'll be able to offer somethin' helpful."

"That's nice of you."

"Well, if Margie isn't gonna come out of our room, what else is there for me to do?"

They finished up their dinners by stepping out in front of the hotel with cigars.

"Who would have it in for Dillon and want to sabotage his boat?" Jerry asked.

"I'm afraid that's a long list," Clint said. "You see, everything Dean does isn't always on the up-and-up."

"Oh, I see."

"This was supposed to be a legitimate enterprise for him, but now I don't know."

"You think he was pulling something?" Jerry asked. "But he had a huge investment in that boat."

"I know his investors had huge investments in the boat," Clint said. "I don't know how much money Dean invested himself."

"But look at the boat he built," Jerry said.

"Yeah," Clint said, "big and heavy. Is it insured? Will he get any money for the fact that it burned and sank? And will his investors get any of that?"

"You think he built this huge boat just to bilk his investors?"

"I don't know, Jerry," Clint said, tapping ash from his cigar, "I just don't know."

TWENTY-SIX

Jerry went back to his room to see how his wife was doing. Clint remained out in front of the hotel, finishing his cigar and thinking. Would Dean Dillon have invited him onto the *Dolly Madison* knowing that it was going to sink? Would he have risked the life of all those people for a scam? He'd known Dillon to con people out of their money, but he'd never known the man to risk the lives of others.

He wondered what had happened to the Warrant brothers. And what about the gamblers, Kingdom and Galvin? And Galvin's woman, Kathy? Clint still didn't know how many people had been picked up from both shores. Maybe he'd find out tomorrow, when he went down to the offices of the Anchor Line to see Stan McKay.

He was about to toss the remainder of the cigar into the street when Angela came walking out the front door.

"I was wondering where you were," she said to him.

"I figured you needed your rest," he said. "How are you?"

"I'm okay," she said. "I have something to talk to you about, though."

"What's that?"

"It's about the *Dolly Madison.*"

"Do you know something about the boat sinking?" he asked.

"Not exactly."

He tossed the cigar into the street after all, and turned to face her.

"Angela, if you know something . . . Was Dean trying to pull something?"

"I don't know about that," she said. "I know something about . . . the cargo."

"What about it?"

"There's something on the boat that's very . . . valuable."

"What do you mean, valuable?"

"I mean worth," she looked around, then lowered her voice and said, "a lot of money."

"I know what valuable means, Angela," Clint said. "You're not being very clear."

"I know it," she said. "I'm taking a big chance talking to you like this, Clint."

"What kind of chance?"

"With my life."

"Well then, maybe we shouldn't be having this conversation outside," he said.

"Your room?" she asked.

"Let's go inside and have some coffee instead," he said.

The man standing in the shadows across the street watched Clint take Angela's arm and lead her back into the hotel. He didn't know if he could still trust Angela or not. He didn't care if she went to bed with the Gunsmith. He just didn't want her talking to him.

Not about what was in the hold of the *Dolly Madison.*

Clint and Angela were seated, and then ordered not only coffee but pie. The waiter did not comment on the fact that Clint had just left the restaurant.

"Okay," Clint said, when they had coffee and pie in front of them, "what's going on, Angela?"

She took a bite of apple pie and a sip of coffee. Clint knew she was gathering her thoughts, and he allowed her to do so in her own time.

"Okay," she said, "I'm just gonna say it."

"Good."

She took a deep breath.

"There's gold on the *Dolly Madison.*"

TWENTY-SEVEN

"Say that again, slowly," Clint said.

"Gold," she said. "On the *Dolly Madison*."

"How do you know?"

"I'll tell you that later," she said.

"Did Dean know about the gold?"

"No," she said. "All he knows is that he was carry-ing some cargo."

"What's the gold in?"

"A big crate."

"Who shipped it?"

"I can't tell you that right now."

"Why not?"

"Well . . ."

"Is the gold stolen?"

She looked at him, surprised "Why would you ask that?"

"Because you don't want to tell me where it came

from, or who shipped it. What else could the answer be?"

"Well, yes," she said, "it was stolen, but it was stolen from somebody who can't report it stolen."

"Which means what, exactly?"

"Which means," she said, "it's up for grabs."

"Oh, I see," he said. "And you want me to help you grab it."

"Why not?" she asked, with a shrug. "I think a lot of people will be trying."

"A lot of people know about this gold?"

"Well . . . not a lot . . ."

"But enough that you think there's going to be a scramble for it," he said. "And you think you'll have an advantage if I help you."

"Yes," she said, "yes, I do think that."

Clint didn't answer right away. His first instinct was to say no, but he didn't usually make a decision until he had all the facts—and at that moment, he didn't have them.

"So?" she asked.

"I'll need to know a lot more," he said.

"What are you going to be doing tomorrow?"

"I was going back downriver to the *Dolly Madison* to do some salvage, and to see what it would take to get her out of there. There'll be some people from the Anchor Line, as well as an engineer. Not to mention the law."

"The law," she said. "You can't let them find that gold."

"Why not?" he asked. "They won't know it's stolen. They'll just think somebody was shipping it up-river."

"No, they won't."

"Why not?"

She bit her lip, then said, "There's too much of it."

"Just how much gold is there, Angela?"

"A lot."

"Wait a minute," he said. "I saw a real heavy crate being loaded just at the end there, after we boarded. Was that it?"

She nodded. "That was it."

"That crate wasn't *filled* with gold, was it?"

"Well," she said, "not filled."

Clint pushed away his unfinished pie and slapped his napkin down on the table. "Angela, I need to know a lot more."

"Like what?"

"Like who shipped the gold? Where did it come from? Who stole it? And how do you know about all of this?"

"All that?"

He nodded. "All that."

Angela pushed away the last bite of her pie.

Clint walked Angela up to the second floor and to her door.

"Would you like to come in?" she asked.

"I don't think so, Angela. I think we both need to get some rest," he said, "and you need to do some heavy thinking."

She nodded.

"All right," she said. "Good night, Clint."

"Good night, Angela."

She unlocked her door and went inside. She reached for the gas lamp in the wall, and as she turned it up saw the man sitting on her bed with his ankles crossed.

"Hello, babe," he said.

Clint went down the hall to his own room, unlocked the door, and turned up the wall lamp as Angela had done. By that light he also saw someone waiting for him on his bed, only it wasn't a man.

"Hello, Clint," Ava said.

TWENTY-EIGHT

"Hello, Ava," he said. "I thought you were staying with your family tonight?"

"Well," she said. "They're not really family. I mean, it's a cousin of my mother's cousin. I can't really figure that out, can you?"

"No," he said, "I don't even think I'll try."

She was lying on top of the bedclothes, still fully attired in a blue dress, which she had pulled up so that her bare legs showed. Her arms were also bare.

"Where've you been?"

"Getting something to eat, and smoking a cigar," he said, "both with a friend."

"What friend?"

"Jerry Sumner," he said. "An engineer who was on the *Dolly Madison*. You ended up on the Louisiana shore, didn't you?"

"That's right?"

"Were you hurt?"

"No," she said. "It was Dean who got me into the water."

"Did you see what happened to Dean?"

"No," she said. "He was supposed to jump off the boat when I did, but he didn't. He made sure I got off, and then I didn't see him again. I figured he thought of something that kept him from leaving."

Something like gold? Clint wondered. Even if he had known about the gold, there was nothing that could have been done while the boat was going down. Even if they were gold bricks, you couldn't have swum to shore with even one.

"What about the Warrant brothers?"

"We never saw them," she said. "Dean was wonderin' where they got to."

"And the gamblers? Kingdom? Galvin?"

"Never saw them. Or the girl, Kathy. They weren't on shore across the river?"

"I don't know," he said. "They weren't there when I was, and I haven't seen everyone who was rescued from there."

"Well," she said, "I guess my job singing on the *Dolly* is over."

"I guess so."

"Think I can get paid?"

"Even if we find Dean," Clint said, "I don't know if he'll have any money. His investors are going to be looking for him."

"I knew it was too good to be true," she said.

"Lots of things are," he said.

"And," she said, pulling the hem of her dress even higher, "others aren't."

* * *

Angela stared at the man on her bed.

"What are you doing here?" she asked. "Did anybody see you?"

"Don't worry," he said. "Nobody saw me."

"Why did you take the chance?"

"I'll tell you why, sweetie," he said. "Because you got me to ship my gold upriver on a boat that sank."

"It shouldn't have sunk," she said, shaking her head. "It was supposed to be impossible."

"When are you gonna learn that nothin' is impossible?" he asked.

She shook her head again, walked to the bed, and sat at the bottom. He slid down to put his arms around her.

"Have you missed me?" he asked, nuzzling her neck.

"Of course," she said, thinking how lucky it was that Clint had not come into the room with her.

"Have you talked to anybody?" he asked. "About the gold?"

"No."

He grabbed her hair and pulled her head back so that her neck was stretched out.

"Are you sure?" he asked in her ear.

"Yes, yes, I'm sure!" she said. "You're hurting me!"

"I'll do worse than that if you tell anyone about it, Angela," he said, releasing her head. "Remember that."

He got off the bed and moved toward the door. "I'd like to spend the night with you, but I've got to make plans to recover that gold." He opened the door and pulled his jacket on. "Remember what I said, Angela."

He held his finger to his lips and slipped into the hall.

Ava slid off her dress and beckoned Clint to the bed with her. He made sure the door was locked, then unbuckled his gun belt, hung it on the bedpost, and got undressed.

Naked, he got into bed with her. She took him in her arms.

"You always make sure that gun is near," she said.

"That's why I'm alive to make love to you," he said.

"Well," she said, "I'm sure not gonna complain about that."

TWENTY-NINE

Clint and Ava entwined their legs and pressed their naked bodies together as they kissed. She slid her hand down between them to massage his hard cock, and he slid his fingers in and out of her wet pussy. They enflamed each other with kisses and touches until Clint slipped a leg over her, straddled her, and slid his cock deep into her. As he fucked her, Ava wrapped her muscular legs and thighs around him, scratched his back with her nails, and bit his shoulder. It was as if she was determined to mark her territory.

Clint grunted and groaned as he drove himself into her, cupping her gorgeous ass in his hands and pulling her onto him with each thrust.

Ava laughed, groaned, and growled as he continued to plow into her. She also exhorted him with cries of "Harder, oh, harder, come on . . ."

The bed began to leap off the floor as their bodies slammed together, as they each strained for release.

Ava's came first, and she dug her nails into him as waves of pleasure rolled over her. Just moments later Clint cried out as he ejaculated into her in powerful, almost painful spurts . . .

"That was just fucking," she said, later, "plain and simple . . ."

They were lying together, her head on his shoulder, perspiration drying on their skin.

"Are you complaining?" he asked.

"Oh, no," she replied. "I'm just sayin' you promised me some lovemaking, and that was fuckin'."

"That's not very ladylike," he told her.

She laughed. "Sugar, ain't you learned by now I ain't very ladylike when I'm in bed with a man?" She made circles on his belly with her fingernails, then stroked his penis. "I'm just sayin' don't get too comfortable, because you ain't finished with me yet, and I definitely ain't finished with you."

"That suits me fine," he said.

She stretched, her breasts growing taut, and added, "But first we'll take a little nap."

"That suits me, too."

They woke hours later and made love more slowly and gently, then slept again. The next time they woke, sunlight was streaming into the room.

"Mornin'," she said, kissing him.

"Good morning." He kissed her lips, her chin, her neck, then lingered around her breasts until her nipples were turgid.

"That's enough," she said, pushing him away. "I need a bath. I smell like a goat."

"You smell fine to me," he said, licking her shoulder. "And you taste good."

She pushed him away again and said, "I need a bath."

"Then go take one."

"This is your room, your hotel, not mine" she said. "You have to arrange a bath."

"Okay, okay," he said, "we'll take a bath."

"Together?" she asked excitedly.

"If they have a tub big enough," he said, "together."

"I think we can fit into a normal tub together," she said, "but you'll have to wash my back."

"I'll wash your back, but then I have to have breakfast," he said.

"I'm sure by then we'll have an appetite," she said.

He got dressed and went down to arrange for the bath.

Fresh from their bath—which took half an hour and lasted until half the tepid water was on the floor—they went across the street to have breakfast in a small café recommended by the desk clerk.

"Very fahn grits," he'd said in his Southern accent.

Clint wasn't crazy about grits, but he did like biscuits and gravy with his steak and eggs.

"What are you gonna do today?" Ava asked, then said, "Oh, that's right. The boat."

"If Dean's body is out there, I'd like to find it," he said.

"I hope he's alive," she said.

"So do I."

In fact, after breakfast he went to the temporary hospital/shelter they'd erected for the survivors. It was a huge tent filled with cots and tables, and as he entered, the survivors were enjoying a breakfast supplied to them by a local restaurant.

Clint recognized some of the people from the boat, but most of the passengers were strangers to him, since there had been so many on board. But there was not even close to the full complement of guests in that tent. He knew that some, like him and Jerry, had been able to make their own arrangements for shelter, but still others were simply not there at all. Their bodies were either at the bottom of the river, still floating on top, or had washed up on shore.

Having satisfied himself that Dean Dillon was not there, he left the tent and walked to the docks, to the offices of the Anchor Line.

THIRTY

Fred Ward and Stan McKay looked up as Clint entered the office.

"Good morning, Adams," Ward said.

"Morning," Clint said, exchanging nods with McKay.

"Ready to go?" Ward asked.

"I'm ready."

"I hope you don't find your friend out there," Ward said.

"I hope to find him alive, somewhere," Clint said.

The door opened again and Jerry Sumner entered. They exchanged greetings and Ward said, "Thank you for offering your expertise on this, Mr. Sumner."

"My pleasure, Mr. Ward," Jerry said. "I'm anxious to find out what happened."

"We all are," Ward said. "Mr. McKay will take you both to the boat."

McKay nodded and led the way out of the office.

"We'll take one flat-bottomed boat today," he told them.

"Will we be picking up bodies?" Clint asked.

"No," McKay said, "that's up to the law. The chief is making arrangements for that. We're just going out today to examine the boat. We'll have two of my men with me who can do the underwater work."

As they reached the boat, Clint saw that, in addition to the two divers McKay talked about, there were several other crewmen.

They got on board and headed downriver. Clint and Jerry sat in the back of the boat, out of the way, and talked.

They had both gone to the temporary shelter to see who was there. Jerry had recognized more people than Clint had, but neither of them had seen any sign of Dean Dillon, Galvin and his woman Kathy, or Kingdom.

"They're out there somewhere," Clint said.

"Yeah, but dead or alive?" Jerry asked.

McKay came back and sat with them.

"When will something be done to salvage the boat?" Clint asked.

"We need to have an owner on hand before anything can be done," McKay said. "If we don't find Dean Dillon, then someone from New Orleans—perhaps an investor—will have to come to town and make arrangements."

"I see."

"Were you friends with Dillon?"

Rather than trying to explain their relationship Clint simply said, "Yes."

"But not an investor?"

"No."

"Were you asked?"

"No, and if I had been I would have said no."

"Why?"

"Same reasons everyone else has been talking about," Clint said. "Too big, and too heavy."

"Dillon is lucky he had Captain Hatton in the wheelhouse," McKay said. "That old warrior saved that boat by getting it to shallow water."

"He doesn't like people very much, does he?" Clint asked.

McKay laughed. "He should never come in off the water," he said. "No, he doesn't have much use for people, unless they're his crewmen."

McKay left them and moved to the front of the boat again.

"Doesn't sound like Dillon's going to have anyone to blame," Jerry said.

"Unless it *was* sabotage," Clint said. "There *was* an explosion, and it didn't come from the steam engines."

"Maybe we'll know more by the end of today," Jerry offered.

"I hope so."

When they reached the *Dolly Madison*, Clint looked around carefully, studying both shores. He wasn't looking for survivors or bodies. If Angela was right about the gold on the boat, and if anyone else knew about it, somebody might have already been there to try to salvage it. But they'd need a hell of a boat if there was as much gold as she'd indicated.

He didn't see anyone about as they pulled up along-side the huge riverboat.

McKay and his men, along with Jerry, went to work belowdecks while Clint took another look around the upper decks to see if anyone was around. After a careful search he determined no one else was on board, and it didn't look like anyone had been there trying to salvage anything. Not yet, anyway.

He went back down to the lower deck, where he waded to where the men were working.

McKay and Jerry was standing there, waiting for the two men who were underwater.

"We can't find anything other than that hole that was blown in the side," McKay said. "Definitely looks like it was done deliberately."

"Have your men taken a look at the cargo hold?" Clint asked.

"No, why would we?"

"Just to be thorough."

McKay didn't seem to understand that. "Are you askin' me to have my men lookin' at the hold for some reason?"

"Nope," Clint said, "I'm just asking questions. Maybe my questions are uninformed."

"I think they might be," McKay said.

"I wish I could get down there to take a look," Jerry said. "I think I'm a little too old to be diving, though."

"Maybe you can get a look from the outside," McKay said. "We can take the boat around to that side."

Clint doubted that. It seemed to him that if the hole

was underwater, Jerry wouldn't be able to examine it whether he was inside or outside.

But then again, he kept his mouth shut because he was uninformed.

THIRTY-ONE

Watching from shore, careful to stay under cover, were three men.

"What if they're there for the gold?" one of them asked.

"They're not," the leader said. He was the man who had been in Angela's room.

"How can you tell?" the third man asked.

"They're not outfitted to salvage it."

"We ain't either," the first man said. "We need a big boat."

"We don't need a boat," the leader said. "The captain managed to get that boat right in the perfect spot for us. We're gonna salvage that gold from shore. We ain't lookin' to float upriver with it."

"How we gonna take it then?"

"We'll need a strong buckboard and a good team," the man said.

"How we gonna get it from the water to the shore?" the first man said.

"That," the leader said, "is somethin' I'm still workin' on."

Clint went up to the wheelhouse to see what Captain Hatton had seen when he was operating the *Dolly Madison*. From there he once again took a long look at both shores, and was about to leave the bridge when he thought he saw something on the Louisiana side. He stared and kept staring, until he saw it again. The glint of sun off of something. He remained where he was until he saw it yet again, and then he was sure.

They were being watched from shore.

He thought about bringing this to the attention of McKay and Jerry Sumner, but then thought again. What would be the point? They weren't concerned with anything but the condition of the boat. What did they care if they were being watched?

In fact, Clint wouldn't have cared, either, except that Angela had told him about the gold. The whole point of blowing a hole in the side of the boat and sinking it might have been to steal the gold. Maybe the thieves were watching, waiting for their chance to swoop in and grab it.

Only how would they do that? If Angela was right about how much there was, it would take a lot of men to get it out of the water and either into another boat or to the shore.

Clint left the wheelhouse and headed back down to the first deck.

*   *   *

He found McKay standing on the deck while his two men were taking Jerry on the flatboat to see what he could see of the *Dolly*'s damage from the outside.

"McKay," he asked, "am I correct that it would be quicker to get here from Vicksburg on horseback than by the river?"

"Definitely," McKay said. "With all the twists and turns in the river, a man on a horse or even on a buckboard would get here much faster."

"That's what I thought."

"Why?"

"Oh, just satisfying myself that I was right," Clint said.

McKay shrugged the question off and walked to the port side of the boat to look down at his men and Jerry.

THIRTY-TWO

"What about a guard?" Clint asked McKay when it was time for them to leave.

"Whataya mean?"

"I mean leaving somebody here with a gun to guard the boat."

"What for? Nobody can steal the boat."

"Yeah, but what about the cargo?"

"Is there something in the cargo that's worth stealin'?" McKay asked.

"I don't know," Clint lied. "But what about the boat being stripped? There are some expensive furnishings on board."

"I can't worry about that, Adams," McKay said. "That's for the law, or the owner, to worry about. My job is done and I have to go back and make my report."

"That's fine," Clint said.

McKay and his men stepped from the *Dolly Madison* to the flatboat, followed by Jerry and Clint.

Once on the boat, Clint took another look over at the Louisiana shoreline to see if he could spot the watchers.

"What are you lookin' for?" Jerry asked.

"I thought I saw something on shore."

"Survivors?"

"I don't know," Clint said. "Just a glint."

"Maybe when we get back, you can have somebody take a look."

"Yeah, maybe."

They didn't talk about it the rest of the way.

When they got to Vicksburg, they split up. Jerry went back to the Anchor Line offices with McKay and his men to make a report. Clint went back to his hotel, but he didn't go to his own room. He went to Angela's. When she opened her door to his knock, she looked relieved.

"I've been lookin' for you," she said.

"Well, here I am."

"Come on in before somebody sees you," she said, grabbing the front of his shirt and pulling him inside. She slammed the door and turned to face him.

"I've decided to tell you the truth," she said.

"All of it?" he asked.

She didn't answer.

"It's not going to work unless you tell me the whole truth, Angela."

"All right," she said, "all of it."

He sat on the bed. "Go ahead."

"Can't you buy me somethin' to eat while we talk? I've been lookin' for you all day."

He realized he was hungry from his day on the river. "All right, let's go across the street—that is, if you're not afraid to be seen with me."

"I'll take the chance," she said. "I'm that hungry."

They went to the same café and ordered two steak dinners.

"All right," he said while they were waiting. "Talk."

She poured them each a cup of coffee from the pot on the table.

"His name is Tate Barnum," she said. "He found out about the gold being shipped upriver on the *Dolly Madison*. It was his idea for me to meet Dillon, get him to like me and hire me as a dealer."

"So you could keep an eye on the gold?"

"So I would know everything that was being planned for the boat."

"Do you know who shipped the gold?"

"No," she said, "but Tate said it's stolen, so when we steal it, it can't be reported."

"How does your friend Tate intend to get it off the boat?"

"I don't know."

"Do you know which side of the river he's going to do it from?"

"The Louisiana side, I think."

"I thought I saw somebody watching us from that side today."

"Probably him."

"Does he have men with him?"

"Yes, but I don't know how many."

"You're telling me a lot without telling me a lot, Angela," he said.

"I'm tellin' you all I know, Clint," she said.

"Have you seen Tate since we arrived?"

"Yes," she said. "He was in my room yesterday when I got back."

"And what did he have to say?"

"He threatened me, told me not to say anything to you about the gold. Or to anyone else."

"And why are you telling me?"

She leaned forward. "Because if it's stolen, and he intends to steal it, then we can steal it from him. It ain't illegal."

"Stealing is illegal no matter who does it, Angela," he said. "And no matter who you steal from."

"But Tate said since we didn't take it in the first place—"

"If it's stolen and you know it, you have an obligation to see that it's returned to the rightful owner."

"A legal obligation?" she asked.

He hesitated. He couldn't cite the law word for word.

"Well, a moral one," he said.

"But if it's moral, and it ain't legal, then we could do it."

The waiter came with their steaks.

"Eat your food and let me think about this a little," he said.

He had no intention of stealing the gold—not for himself, anyway. But with her help he could make sure that Tate Barnum didn't get away with it, and that the original thieves didn't, either.

The question was, how?

THIRTY-THREE

After they finished their food and desert, Angela asked, "So what do you think?"

"I think I should go across the river and see what I can see," he replied. "Do you know what town he's in over there?"

"Nearest one, I guess."

"I'll have to find out where that is. What's he look like?"

She described him. Young, tall, handsome.

"If he's all that," he said, "why do you want to join with me and steal the gold from him?"

"Because he's mean," she said. "And because you're the Gunsmith. Workin' with you, I think we can get away with it."

"We'll see about that," he said. "Come on. You better get back to the hotel."

"What are you gonna do?"

"I've got some research to do."

* * *

After leaving her at the hotel, Clint went directly to the nearest telegraph office. He sent two telegrams, one to his friend Rick Hartman in Labyrinth, Texas, and one to his private detective friend, Talbot Roper, in San Francisco. Both men had extensive networks across the country that they could get information from. Clint asked them to find out anything they could about the theft of a large amount of gold.

After leaving the telegraph office, he walked to the police station. Chief Radcliffe saw Clint in his office and offered him some coffee.

"Thanks, Chief."

Radcliffe poured two cups, carried them back to his desk, and handed Clint one.

"What's on your mind, Mr. Adams?"

"Louisiana, Chief," Clint said. "What town is across the river from here? And I mean a town of some size."

"That'd be Bedford. Not a big town."

"Are you familiar with the law in that town?"

"Sure. Sheriff Toby Farrell."

"Good man?"

"Not so much."

"Honest?"

"As the day is long. Why?"

"I think I might be needing his help," Clint said.

"Does this have to do with the *Dolly Madison*?" the chief asked.

"It might," Clint said. "I can't be sure right now, but it might. All I know right now is that I'll be going across the river tomorrow to talk to him."

"And you want me to vouch for you?"

"I wouldn't ask you to do that," Clint said. "You just met me. I'll stand on my reputation."

"Well, you just have Toby send me a telegram if he wants," the chief said. "I'll put in a good word."

"Thank you, Chief. I appreciate it."

"Sure thing."

Clint left the police station and went back to his hotel. He stopped outside the door to his room, thought about going down to Angela's, then changed his mind. He put the key in his lock and hoped that nobody was on the other side when he opened it. He was tired from a day on the river.

Bone tired.

THIRTY-FOUR

Clint woke the next morning refreshed, and with a revelation.

As he dressed and went downstairs for breakfast, choosing to eat in the hotel today, he went over it again and again in his mind, and he was sure that he was right.

It made no sense for anyone who wanted to steal the gold to sink the boat. How could you get that much gold up from the bottom of the Mississippi? Unless, of course, you knew that the boat was going to sink in three feet of water.

Of course, it hadn't sunk in three feet, but it had definitely not been completely immersed in the waters of the river. The gold might or might not be salvageable from where it was now. The point he had come to was that this job could not have been pulled off without the cooperation of the captain. He was the man whose job it was to make sure the boat went down in shallow water. No one else could have done it.

So, after breakfast, Clint decided that instead of going to Louisiana, all he had to do was find the captain and take him to the chief of police. Of course, when he prevented the gold from being stolen, Angela was not going to be happy, but he'd deal with that when the time came. She couldn't really believe that he was going to help her steal the gold, could she? Did she really believe that stealing something that had already been stolen wasn't stealing?

He wondered when the bodies of the dead would start to be brought to town, and wondered if they'd do that by the river or by buckboard. He was still hoping Dean Dillon was alive. Whatever Dillon's scam was, he certainly deserved to have to deal with the consequences if he *was* alive.

Clint went to the offices of the Anchor Line to see if Fred Ward or Stan McKay could tell him where to find Captain Hatton. Both men were there.

"What do you want with him?" Ward asked.

"I just have a few questions."

"I think he's staying at a hotel here near the docks," Ward said. "Stan?"

"Yeah, I know where he is, but he ain't gonna be too happy to see you, Adams."

"What's he got against me?"

"Not you," McKay said, "people. Landlubbers. You qualify on both counts."

"Will you take me to see him?" Clint asked.

"Sure, why not?"

"Don't be gone too long, Stan," Ward said.

"I'll just walk Adams over there and make sure the captain doesn't try to take his head off."

"Much obliged," Clint said.

It was a run-down hotel patronized by dockworkers, crewmen from riverboats, and Captain Hatton.

"Hatton?" the desk clerk said. "Yeah, he's here, room five, right back there."

There was a hallway on the first floor, straight back. Clint and McKay headed down the hall.

When they got to room five, Clint knocked, waited, then knocked again. He looked at McKay.

"Maybe he's drunk," McKay said. "Or he just doesn't want to answer."

Clint tried the doorknob. It turned freely.

"Hey!" McKay said.

"Would the captain leave his room unlocked?"

"Well . . . no, probably not."

Clint pushed the door open and stepped into the room. The captain was lying on his back on the bed.

"See?" McKay said. "Drunk."

"I don't smell any liquor," Clint said. "On the other hand, I do smell blood."

"What?"

Clint approached the bed. The mattress was soaked with Hatton's blood.

"Is he dead?" McKay asked, shocked.

"Couldn't be deader. You better go downstairs and send for the police."

"Okay. Jesus, how was he killed?"

"Looks to me like a knife wound," Clint said, staring at the body. "A lot of knife wounds."

"Jesus."

"Go ahead, Stan," Clint said. "Get the police. I think Chief Radcliffe will be very interested in this."

"Interested in what?"

"A little story I have to tell him," Clint said. "Come on, get going!"

THIRTY-FIVE

Chief Radcliffe looked down at the body of Captain Hatton.

"You know anything about this?" he asked Clint.

"I walked in and found him. That's all I know."

"Stan McKay seems to think you have a story to tell me."

Slip of the tongue, Clint thought. Did he want to tell Radcliffe about the gold? Maybe he could make his point without it.

"I came here to ask Hatton some questions."

"What kind of questions?"

"About the boat sinking," Clint said. "About him getting the boat someplace where it wouldn't sink completely."

"You think the captain had something to do with sinking the boat?"

"I think he was supposed to get the boat someplace

where it was a lot more shallow, only he didn't make it."

"Why?"

"So somebody could get something off the boat with no trouble."

"Blowing a boat up and sinking it is no trouble?" Radcliffe asked.

"Sinking that boat in three feet of water would have caused no trouble for anybody but Dillon and his investors. Somebody could have come along on a boat and taken what they wanted."

"Like what?"

"I don't know what's on the boat, Chief," Clint said. "You'd have to ask Dillon that."

"Or take a look."

"You'd have to dive to do that, or raise the boat. And then look in every crate."

"Isn't there a manifest?"

"I wouldn't know where that is."

Radcliffe looked down at Hatton's body.

"Murder," the chief said. "I hate murder. I'm no detective."

"Hire one," Clint said. "Put him on your payroll."

"What about you?" the chief asked. "You want the job?"

"I'm not a detective."

"I get the feeling you're a lot of things, Adams."

"You need a real detective," Clint said.

"Yeah, I guess I do. Meanwhile, I'll have the body moved, talk to his men."

"His men?"

"His copilot, crewman. I understand he had two of them with him, and that Dillon hired the rest."

"Cheap labor," Clint said. "They ran—or swam—when the fire started."

"Why start a fire?" Chief asked.

"I don't think that was intentional," Clint said. "I think the whole plan went bad as soon as the explosion went off—and I think that happened earlier than planned."

"What about Dillon?"

"What about him?"

"He's nowhere to be found," Radcliffe said. "Could he be behind the whole thing?"

"He could be dead."

"That wouldn't make him innocent."

"You're right, it wouldn't."

"You're gonna look for him, aren't you?"

"Yes."

"I thought you weren't a detective?"

"You don't have to be a detective to track a man down."

"If you come across any information I should have, you'll tell me, right?"

"You'll be the first, Chief"

They had to get out of the room so the doctor could come in, as well as the men who would be carrying the body out. They reconvened in front of the hotel, where a bit of a crowd had gathered to try and find out what happened, or maybe see some blood.

"So the last time we talked, you weren't thinking

about Captain Hatton as a conspirator?" the chief asked.

"No," Clint said, "I woke up this morning with that thought in my head and decided to follow it up by having a talk with him. I went to the Anchor Line to see if they could help me find him. McKay said he knew where Hatton was staying, and here we are."

The chief scratched his head as the captain's body was carried out on a stretcher, covered with a sheet that was soaked through with his blood. The crowd was getting what they wanted.

"Remember," the chief said, "anything you find out, you let me know."

"You got my word, Chief," Clint assured the man.

THIRTY-SIX

After Clint left the chief, he rented a horse from a stable in Vicksburg and rode it over to his hotel. He went to his room, retrieved his rifle, and carried it back downstairs. When he reached the horse, Angela was there, sitting on another horse right beside it.

"What's going on?" he asked.

"I'm going with you."

"Where?"

"After the gold."

"What makes you think I'm going after the gold?" he asked.

"Why wouldn't you?" she asked. "It's gold."

He stared up at her.

"All right, then, where are you planning on going?" she asked.

"Bedford."

"What's in Bedford?"

He mounted his horse.

"That's what we're going to find out."

They used the Old Vicksburg Bridge to cross over to the Louisiana side, then rode south to Bedford.

"What's so interestin' about Bedford?" Angela asked.

"It's the nearest town to where the boat sank," he said. "It's also the closest Louisiana town to Vicksburg."

"So?"

"Somebody was watching us from the shore when we went to the boat yesterday," he said. "I'm figuring whoever it was came from Bedford."

"Why not Vicksburg?" she asked. "It's bigger."

"Wrong side of the river."

They rode a little farther and then she asked, "Can I have a gun?"

"No."

As they entered Bedford, Clint thought it shouldn't be too hard to find the men he was looking for. Bedford was a pimple on the ass of Vicksburg.

He spotted the sheriff's office right away and rode over to it.

"Stay here with the horses," he said.

"Why?"

"You asked me if you could come along," he said, "so now you have to do as you're told."

He could see she wanted to argue, but he didn't give her the chance. He mounted the boardwalk and entered the sheriff's office.

The man in the office looked up from his desk. He had a sheriff's badge pinned to the front of a soiled shirt. He had long, dirty black hair and looked about forty. He was also eating chicken, the grease shiny on his hands and face.

"Help ya?"

"You Sheriff Farrell?"

"That's me."

"My name's Clint Adams."

"The Gunsmith?"

"Yes."

Farrell looked unconcerned. He dropped the chicken leg he was eating. Clint was afraid he was going to offer to shake hands, but he didn't. He just wiped his hand on his shirt.

"What can I do for you?"

Clint explained about the *Dolly Madison* and why he was in Bedford.

"I heard about that boat goin' down."

"Any strangers in town lately?"

"Yeah, as a matter of fact," the sheriff said. "Three."

"Where are they?"

"I don't know," Farrell said. "They had a room at the hotel, but I don't know if they're still there."

"Any place in town to rent a buckboard?"

"Sure, the livery."

"I'll check over there, then."

"What then?"

"I'm going to take a ride out to the site where the boat went down."

"Want me to go with ya?" Farrell asked.

"No," Clint said, "that's okay. I'm just going out to take a look."

"You expectin' these three to be lootin' the boat?" Farrell asked.

"It's possible."

"You an owner?"

"No," I said, "but I'm friends with the owner."

Farrell picked up his chicken again and said, "Close enough."

THIRTY-SEVEN

"Yeah, I rented out a buckboard, but it was a funny thing," the fat liveryman said.

"What?" Clint asked.

"They wanted me to reinforce it," the man said. "Like they was gonna be haulin' somethin' real heavy."

Clint turned his head and looked out through the front door to where Angela was waiting with the horses again.

"Did you do the work?"

"Oh yeah, and I did a good job, too."

"When did they pick it up?"

"Yesterday afternoon."

"Did they leave town with it?"

"I think so. Leastways, I ain't seen them since."

"Any names?"

"Naw," the man said. "I didn't need names to do the job. And they paid me in advance."

"Okay," Clint said. "Thanks."

They went to the hotel next, and once again Angela stayed outside.

"No, sir, they ain't checked out yet," the clerk said.

"Okay, thanks." Clint turned to leave, then turned back. "Oh, one thing. If they come back, don't tell them anyone was asking for them."

"If they come back?"

"Yeah," Clint said, "they may not be able to. Understand?"

The young clerk swallowed and nodded. Clint walked out.

"Where are we goin' now?" Angela asked as they rode out of town. They had been there for half an hour.

"Out to the boat."

"Are we gonna get the gold?"

He looked at her.

"Where would we put it?" he asked. "In our saddlebags?"

"So then we'll just let them bring it up, and we'll take it from them?"

"Let's see what happens when we get there," he said.

The two men came up from the depths of the Mississippi and gulped for air. The third man—the leader—looked down at them from the first deck of the *Dolly*.

"What the hell are you comin up for?" he demanded.

"We gotta breathe!"

The leader put his foot on one of their heads and pushed him back underwater.

"You can breathe when you tell me somethin' about the gold!" he yelled. "Understand?"

The other man said, "Yeah, we understand."

The leader removed his foot so the other man could take a breath, and then both men dove.

Clint and Angela rode along the shore until they came to the buckboard and two horses. Out on the river they could see the *Dolly Madison*.

"They don't have it yet," she said. "The buckboard's empty."

"Shhh," he said, trying to quiet her. "Dismount."

They tied their horses off so they wouldn't wander away, then moved closer to the shore while staying hidden behind the brush.

"I don't see anybody," Angela said, keeping her voice low.

"If they're trying to get to the gold, they're probably on the other side of the boat," Clint explained. "Keep quiet and listen."

They both fell silent, and before long they were able to hear voices—or, rather, one voice, and an angry one at that.

"That sound familiar?" he asked her.

"Unfortunately," she said, "yes." She made a face. "Nobody you know."

"Not Dean? Not Kingdom?"

"No, no," she said, "I told you, it's nobody you know."

"Well, maybe it's somebody I should meet."

"His name is Kevin, Kevin DuBois."

"DuBois?"

She nodded.

"He's my husband."

THIRTY-EIGHT

"Your what?"

She looked away.

"My husband."

"Why didn't you tell me that before?"

"I didn't think it was that important."

"So are you setting me up here for him?" Clint asked.

"No," she said, "I'm tryin' to set him up for you."

"Your husband."

"Well, we're married," she said, "but we're not a happy couple. I'm tryin' to get away from him, and he said if I helped him steal the gold he'd let me go."

"Do you know who he's got with him? Or how many?"

"I think he's got two men, but I don't know who they are," she said. "I'm pretty sure he means to stiff them, though. Get them to do the work and then take off with the gold."

"Kill them?"

"I'm not sure," she said. "Maybe."

"Can he handle a gun?"

"Yes, he's good with a gun."

"And he probably hired two men who aren't," Clint said. "Tell me, does Dean Dillon know your husband?"

"No, they've never met."

Clint turned his head to look out at the *Dolly Madison* again.

"What are you thinkin'?" Angela asked.

"I don't see how they can take any gold off that boat," he said. "Not without some kind of special equipment. Is it in gold bars?"

"I don't know," she said. "It could be."

"They could take it off several bars at a time," Clint said, "but that would take forever. Is he determined to take all of it?"

"Every bit of it," she said.

Clint shook his head. "Can't be done."

"Kevin is stubborn," she said.

They'd need a boat, Clint thought. Of course, there could be a boat out there alongside the *Dolly Madison*, but it wouldn't be large enough or strong enough to take all the gold.

Clint assumed that all the bodies had been picked up from both shores or plucked out of the water. The only reason for anyone else to come back would be to pull the *Dolly Madison* out of there, but he'd been told that nothing could be done before they found the owner—or someone to replace him. So they probably had a lot of time to get the gold off, and they'd need it.

But time or no time, they just didn't have the equipment.

The two divers came up, again empty-handed.

"Can't get the crate open," one of them said.

"Do you have the right crate?"

"It's the one you described to us, Kevin," the second man said. "But we can't get it open."

Kevin DuBois stared at them for a moment, then looked at the sky and shouted, "Damnit!" He looked at them again. "I didn't blow a hole in this boat and sink it just to come up empty."

"But, Boss, ya can't get the whole crate up," one of them said.

"And we can't get it open," the second man said.

"Then what good are you to me?"

DuBois stood up, drew his gun, and shot each man in the head. They sank beneath the surface with startled looks on their faces.

THIRTY-NINE

Clint and Angela heard the shots.

"What the—" Clint said.

"Oh, no," Angela said.

Clint looked at her.

"He must have decided he doesn't need them anymore," she said.

"He killed his men?" he said. "You knew he was going to kill them."

"Well . . ."

"You're still holding out on me."

She stared at him.

"You have to promise me you'll protect me," she said. "Kevin is a killer. He blew a hole in the boat, not caring if it killed anybody. And on every job he pulls, he kills his men when he doesn't need them anymore. Is that clear enough for you?"

"Is there anything else I should know?"

"No."

"You sure?"

"Positive. Except . . ."

"Except what?" he asked, staring at her.

She pointed out to the water and said, "He's comin' back."

Clint looked out toward the *Dolly Madison* and saw Kevin DuBois coming back in a rowboat.

"Okay, tell me something quickly."

"What?"

"Is Kevin smart?" Clint asked.

"Um, well, yeah . . ."

"Does he plan his own jobs?"

She hesitated.

"Angela?"

"Well, I've always wondered about that."

"What do you mean?"

"I mean once I married him, once I was around him for a while, it seemed to me he wasn't all that smart."

"And?"

She shrugged and said, "His jobs always work out right."

"Except for this one."

"That didn't have to be his fault," she said. "I mean, that explosion could have been premature, right?"

He stared at her. "Would Kevin even know what 'premature' means?"

"No," she said, seeming stunned, "he wouldn't. Oh my God, he's *not* that smart."

Clint nodded "Okay, somebody planned this for him. We need to find out who."

"Why?" she asked. "He's comin' back from the boat now. Just kill him, and then we'll take the gold."

"He was out there with two men, and the three of them couldn't bring up that gold. How are we going to do it?"

"Well, you're smarter than Kevin is."

"But am I smarter than whoever Kevin is working for?"

"I'll bet you are."

"Well," Clint said, "let's find out."

"How do we do that?"

"We find out who it is," Clint said. "And for that we need your Kevin alive."

"Okay," she said, "but promise me one thing."

"What's that?"

"When this is all over," she said, "you'll kill him."

"Why don't you just get a divorce?"

"Because he would kill me before he divorces me."

"How about this?" he asked. "I'll kill him before I let him kill you."

She sighed. "I guess that'll have to do."

They were waiting for him when he got off the boat and dragged it up onto shore. He turned and stopped short when he saw them, flinched as if he was going to go for his gun.

"Whoa," Clint said. "If you do that, you'll die right here."

"Adams?" Kevin asked.

"That's right."

The look DuBois gave his wife was murderous. She,

on the other hand, was willing him to go for his gun. She was disappointed when he stood up straight and moved his hand away from it.

"So what's this?" he asked. "She give you a little something to kill me?"

"She told me about the gold, if that's what you mean."

"Well, it's out there," DuBois said. "Go and get it."

"No. You and your two men weren't able to do that. So now they're at the bottom of the river with the gold. I'd like to know what your next move was going to be."

"Why should I tell you?"

"Okay, I'll tell you," Clint said. "You were going to talk to the man you work for."

DuBois laughed.

"I don't work for anybody," he said. "People work for me."

"Until you kill them."

"Look, you wanna work for me? Fine. Otherwise get out of my way."

"You just killed two men," Clint said. "We saw you do it." DuBois didn't know whether they had actually seen him or not, but that didn't matter. "Why don't we just go talk to the sheriff?"

"You'd do that to me?" DuBois asked. He was talking to Angela, not Clint.

"In a minute," she said.

Now he looked at Clint. "Okay, what do you want?"

"I want to know who you work for," Clint said. "And I want to meet him."

"I can't—"

"You'll have a better chance of getting that gold up with me than without me."

DuBois stared at him.

"Let me put that another way," Clint said. "Without me you have no chance of getting that gold . . . at all."

FORTY

DuBois mounted one of the horses, quite content to leave the other and the buckboard behind.

"No good," Clint said. "You rented the buckboard and the liveryman will be looking for it."

"What the hell—" DuBois said. "Why don't we just ride to Vicksburg?"

"That's where your boss is?" Clint asked.

"That's where my employer is," DuBois said, clearly not comfortable with the word "boss."

"Nevertheless," Clint said, "we better return that buckboard."

"What about the riderless horse?" Angela asked. "Won't that draw attention?"

"You're right," Clint said. "We'll leave it just outside of town where someone will find it. By that time we'll be gone."

Clint didn't think the sheriff would expend much energy trying to find the rider.

Clint allowed DuBois to keep his gun but kept the man in front of him during the ride back. He made Dubois drive the buckboard, with both horses tied to the back. Just outside of town they untied one horse and tied it to a tree, then rode in and returned the buckboard. After that DuBois mounted his horse and they headed for Vicksburg. Clint still kept the man ahead of him, with Angela riding right alongside Clint.

Clint wondered if one of the missing men—Dillon, Kingdom, or Galvin—would turn out to be the "employer"? Or would it be someone else entirely?

"DuBois," he called out.

"Yeah?"

Clint rode up alongside the buckboard.

"Who were the two men you left in the river?" Clint asked.

"Does that matter?"

"It might," Clint said. Might give him a better picture of who he was dealing with.

DuBois gave Clint a scowl, as if he didn't really want to answer the question, then said, "It was Sam and Lou Warrant."

Somehow that didn't surprise Clint at all.

They got back to Vicksburg late in the afternoon and reined in their horses in front of Clint's hotel.

"Where do we find him?" Clint asked.

"Actually," DuBois said, "he usually finds me."

"I don't buy that," Clint said.

"It's true," DuBois said. "I don't know where he stays."

"That may be, but you don't just wait around for

him to find you," Clint said. "There's got to be some-place that you and he leave messages for each other."

Clint could tell by the look on DuBois's face that he was right.

"Well, yeah . . ." DuBois said.

"Where is it?"

DuBois took a breath and blew it out in a gesture of annoyance.

"There's a saloon we use," he finally said.

"Where?"

"It's at the far end—"

"Never mind," Clint said. "You're going to take me there."

"When?"

"Now."

"I'm comin'—" Angela started, but Clint cut her off.

"No, you're going to stay in the hotel," he said. "This might get dangerous."

She made a face, but didn't argue.

"We'll take the horses to the livery, and then you'll take me to the saloon."

DuBois didn't argue, but got a crafty glint in his eye.

"If you try anything," Clint told him, "I'll kill you in a minute."

"In cold blood?" DuBois sneered.

"Hey, you blew a hole in the side of a boat with no thought about the lives it might cost," Clint said. "I won't hesitate to put a bullet in your head."

DuBois suddenly looked less arrogant.

"Let's go," he said, grabbing the reins of Angela's horse. "Go to your room and wait there."

She nodded.

As Clint and DuBois rode toward the livery, Du-
Bois said, "You pokin' that bitch? Is that it?"

"Keep it up, DuBois," Clint said. "Every time you
open your mouth, you give me less and less reason to
keep you alive."

FORTY-ONE

They left the horses at the livery, and then Clint again instructed DuBois to take him to the saloon he and his employer used to leave messages for each other.

"So, you don't know this guy's name?" he asked as they walked.

"No."

"How did you meet?"

"He approached me in New Orleans, told me about the gold, and offered me a cut to help him steal it."

"Do you know who put the gold on the boat?"

"No," DuBois said, "he didn't tell me that."

"You think he knows?"

"Oh, yeah, he knows," DuBois said. "He's takin' a lot of pleasure from stealin' this gold. I think that has to do with who stole it in the first place."

"And does he know who the gold was stolen from?"

"I think he does, yeah."

When they reached the saloon DuBois said, "This is the one."

It was small, kind of run-down, and had a faded and pitted sign over the door that barely said "THE RUSTY SPUR."

"Let's go," Clint said.

"Together?" DuBois said. "You're gonna get me killed."

"You're not afraid of your . . . employer, are you?"

"He's usually got a couple of men with him."

"Okay," Clint said, "you go in and leave a message with the bartender. Tell your man to meet you in an hour."

"What if the bartender can't get the message to him that quick?"

"I'm betting he can."

"What makes you think you can trust me to leave the right message?"

"Because I'm going to write it," Clint said, "and watch you through the window while you hand it to him."

Clint watched as DuBois handed the bartender the note, making sure he didn't have a chance to replace it. When DuBois came out, he asked, "Now what?"

"Now we wait."

"Where?"

Clint pointed across the street.

"Right over there," he said. "Let's go."

FORTY-TWO

They stood across the street for forty-five minutes before DuBois jerked straight and said, "There he is, and he's got two gunhands with him."

Clint saw them, three men entering the saloon.

"I'll be damned," he said.

"You know him?"

"Yeah," Clint said, "and it's not who I thought it would be."

"Who is he?"

"You'll see," Clint said. "Let's go."

They started across, but Clint said, "Wait."

"What for?"

Clint removed DuBois's gun from his holster, ejected all six shells, and then replaced it.

"You can't do that," DuBois said. "I could get killed."

"I just don't want you to get any ideas—like taking sides if there's shooting. Move."

They walked across the street and entered the saloon. The three men had split up. One was seated at a table, the other two were at the bar.

The man at the table looked up and froze when he saw Clint with DuBois.

"What's Adams doing here?" Hal Miller asked. "What's goin' on?"

"He wants in," DuBois said.

"What?"

"He wants a cut of the gold."

"You fool," Miller said, "The Gunsmith's no thief."

"But—"

"Never mind, Kevin," Clint said. "Just stand aside."

DuBois did as he was told.

"Hello, Miller," Clint said. "Can't say I think much of you as an investor, hiring somebody to put a hole in your own boat."

"What makes you think—"

"Too bad you didn't hire somebody who knew what he was doing," Clint went on. "That dynamite went off too soon. At least you did okay when you hired the captain."

Miller sat back in his chair.

"You think I bribed everybody on that boat?" he asked.

"Let's see . . . probably just the captain, and the Warrant brothers. DuBois here, he wasn't on the boat. For a while I thought Dillon, Kingdom, or Galvin might be in it with you, but I'm starting to think they're dead."

"Look, Adams," Miller said, "that gold is up for

grabs. One of my partners, Danny Rawlins, stole that gold. I'm just stealin' it from him."

"And destroying Dean Dillon's unsinkable boat."

"It would have sunk sooner or later," he said. "It's just too damn heavy."

"That may be, but Dean Dillon deserved the chance to make it work."

"You can't imagine how much gold is there, Adams."

"I have to imagine it, Miller, because it's at the bottom of the Mississippi. How were you planning to get it out?"

"That is a problem," Miller said. "The boat was only supposed to go down in three feet of water. I'll tell you what, though. You figure it out, and I'll split it with you, fifty-fifty."

"That's real generous."

"Hey!" DuBois said. "Some of that gold is mine."

Miller produced a gun and shot DuBois in the chest.

"Not anymore," Miller said, as DuBois fell to the floor.

He made a show of holstering the gun in a shoulder rig and then showing Clint his hands.

"What do you say, Adams?" he asked. "Partners?"

"You were right the first time, Miller," Clint said.

"What do you mean?"

"I'm no thief."

FORTY-THREE

Clint kept his eyes on Miller. He didn't think the man would be foolish enough to try and draw on him, but he did have those two men at the bar backing his play.

"Okay, Adams," Miller said, "before this gets out of hand, there's something you should know."

"What?"

"It's about Dillon."

"What about Dean?"

"He's alive."

"You've seen him?"

Miller nodded. "Just a little while ago."

"Where?"

"In town."

"What about Johnny Kingdom and Troy Galvin?" Clint asked.

"I don't know about them, but then I'm not in business with them."

"If Dean is alive, you won't be in business with him much longer, not when he finds out what you did."

"But that's just it," Miller said. "You're not getting it, Adams."

"Then why don't you explain it to me so I do get it, Miller?"

"It's Dillon," Miller said. "He's my partner."

"In the boat?"

"Don't be dense," Miller said. "He was in on the theft of the gold."

"And blowing up his own boat?"

"Well," Miller said, "I admit that part came as a surprise to him, but after I explained it to him he understood. And if he understands, why can't you?"

"I don't believe you, Miller."

"Then ask him yourself."

"Where is he?"

"I'll take you to him," Miller said. "I want to see the two of you together. I want to see your face when you realize your friend conned you."

"Dean and I are not exactly friends," Clint said. "And pulling cons is his life."

"Then why did you agree to go on the boat?"

"I thought maybe, just maybe this time he was on the up-and-up. And when I saw the size of the boat, and figured how much he must have invested in it—"

"Him?" Miller said. "I thought he hadn't invested any of his own money."

"He did, and he also raised the money to build it," Clint said.

"Well, you'll have to take all of that up with him,"

Miller said. He pushed his chair back and stood up. "Shall we go?"

"Lead the way," Clint said. "Only leave your gun-hands here."

"Sure, sure," Miller said. "We're just going to go and have a friendly chat with Dean."

Miller led the way out the batwing doors, with Clint close behind him. They stepped down into the street, and suddenly Miller shouted, "Get him!" and hit the dirt.

Clint turned quickly as the two gunmen came out the batwing doors with their guns out. He fired immediately, hitting both men before they could pull the triggers of their guns.

He turned again, and spotted a man on the roof across the street. The man fired, and Clint felt the breeze as the bullet whizzed by his head. He fired also, and his bullet drilled a hole in the man's forehead. He dropped his rifle, then slipped over the edge himself. The rifle hit the ground just before he did.

Miller was scrambling away, his gun in his hand, but he wasn't in a hurry to use it. He got to his feet and started to run, but Clint shouted, "Hold it!"

Miller froze.

"Your ambush didn't work, Miller."

"What do you mean? I didn't know they were going to pull that."

"Yeah," Clint said, "that's why you yelled 'Get him!'"

"I—I didn't," Miller said. "I yelled . . ." But he was apparently at a loss for a good lie.

"Drop the gun."

He dropped it into the dirt.

"Don't kill me, Adams," he pleaded, turning around. Clint could see the fear on his face—the same fear all those people on the boat must have felt as they were jumping overboard.

"Is Dean alive?" Clint asked.

"I—I don't know," Miller said. "I haven't seen him."

"That's what I thought," Clint said. "A liar and a thief."

"What about Danny Rawlins?" Miller demanded. "He stole the gold first."

"I don't care who stole it first, or who from," Clint said. "None of that means anything to me. You're the one responsible for burning the boat and sinking it. A lot of people got hurt, some died. You're going to pay for that."

"Adams, don't—"

"Turn around and start walking."

"W-where?"

"The police station," Clint said. "You're going to tell the chief of police all about it."

FORTY-FOUR

The next morning Angela was waiting for Clint when he came down to the hotel lobby.

"You killed him," she said.

"No," he said, "Miller killed him."

"And you've been avoiding me."

"I don't think we have anything left to say to each other."

"What about the gold?"

"The chief of police is going to take care of having the gold recovered," Clint said.

"So that's it, then?"

"That's it, Angela," he said. "It'll go back where it belongs."

Clint had found two telegrams waiting for him when he got back to his hotel the night before. Neither Rick Hartman nor Talbot Roper had any information about a gold theft. Apparently, whoever it had been stolen from was keeping it quiet.

"What if nobody claims it?" Clint had asked the chief.

"I'm not sure," the chief said. "Could be if no one claims it in a certain amount of time it would be yours for the claiming."

"Not me," Clint said.

"Well, the way my report is gonna read," the chief said, "you recovered it."

Clint didn't know what to do with that situation, but he certainly wasn't going to tell Angela about it.

"You tried to use me, Angela," he said. "I don't appreciate that."

"I'm sorry, Clint."

"Good-bye," he said, and walked out.

Clint looked out over what seemed to be a sea of covered bodies. The chief had arranged for him to view the bodies in an attempt to find Dean Dillon.

"Be my guest," he was told when he got there. It was a tent that had been erected just for this purpose. "They all gotta be buried today or they're gonna start to smell," an attendant told him.

Clint began to move among them, pulling back the coverings so he could see their faces. Before long he found Johnny Kingdom, the gambler. The body had some burns on it, but Kingdom had apparently drowned. Next, he found Troy Galvin. The *Dolly Madison* sinking had not been kind to gamblers.

He moved through the rest of the bodies. Oddly enough, he did not find Galvin's girlfriend Kathy, and he did not find Dean Dillon.

When he came out of the tent, he found Chief Radcliffe waiting for him.

"Find your friend?" the man asked.

"No."

"That's good, right?"

"Dillon was a con man most of his life, Sheriff," Clint said. "I can't help feeling conned."

"But what did he get out of it?" the chief asked. "He doesn't have the boat, and he doesn't have the gold."

"I don't know," Clint said. "I can't figure it."

The girl was missing, too. Could it be that Dillon wanted the girl?

"We sent a telegram to New Orleans to that name you gave us," the chief said. "William Kennedy?"

"The other investor."

The chief nodded.

"He replied. He'll be down here as soon as he can. Also, we informed the law there about Danny Rawlins. They're lookin' for him."

"That's good."

"What about you?" the chief asked.

"I'll be heading back to Texas," Clint said.

"Not back to New Orleans?"

"No. I've had enough."

He and the chief began walking back toward the police station.

"It's a shame," the chief said. "By all accounts that was a very impressive boat."

"Not impressive enough," Clint said. "People found something else to fight about, to die over."

"Everybody finds something different that's valuable to them."

Clint shook his head. "I really thought for Dean Dillon it was this boat."

"Well," the chief said, "he's not dead. Maybe he'll still show up to claim it."

"He's on the run, I think," Clint said.

"From who?"

"His investors."

"Only one of those left," the chief said.

"He doesn't know that," Clint said.

"Well, maybe you'll run into him again."

When they reached the police station, the chief asked, "So what now? Leaving?"

Clint thought about Ava, back at the hotel. She still didn't know about everything that had happened. And he liked her too much to just leave.

"I do have somebody in town to say good-bye to," he said, "so maybe I'll be leaving tomorrow."

Watch for

WITH DEADLY INTENT

350th novel in the exciting GUNSMITH series
from Jove

Coming in February!

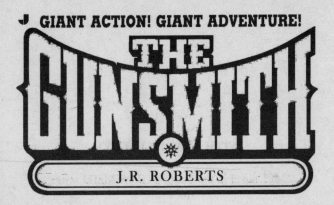

GIANT ACTION! GIANT ADVENTURE!

THE GUNSMITH

J.R. ROBERTS

penguin.com/actionwesterns

M455AS0510